ASPHALT GODS
A WALKING THE WORLDS ADVENTURE

REBECCA BUCHANAN

CONTENTS

~ Author's Note ~ — v

~ One ~ — 1
~ Two ~ — 11
~ Three ~ — 32
~ Four ~ — 45
~ Five ~ — 59
~ Six ~ — 69
~ Epilogue ~ — 86

About the Author — 89

Asphalt Gods was originally published in the online journal *evOke: witchcraft*paganism*lifestyle*, which has since closed. It was later collected as the title story in *Asphalt Gods and Other Pagan Urban Fantasy Tales* (Asphodel Press), which is now *also* out of print. As such, I have opted to publish it as a stand-alone print and ebook as part of my on-going series of interconnected novellas and short stories, *Walking the Worlds*. Those who wish to read more in this series will find them listed on the About the Author page at the end of this book, and on my site, *Eternal Haunted Summer*.

~ ONE ~

There have always been roads.

When the Gods willed themselves into existence, they created pathways, walking the nothingness of potentiality. As they shaped that nothingness into somethingness, they created more pathways: broad boulevards and wide thoroughfares, twisty little tracks and lazy winding lanes.

These roads still exist. Most remain known only to the Gods, but a few — a very few — have been mapped by those species which came to be in the somethingness (how and why we came to be, well, there are as many different explanations for that as there are species).

At any rate, some of us have learned how to travel these roads and, for the most part, the Gods don't seem to mind. They generally approve of curiosity and cleverness. Occasionally, however, we will stumble across a lost or even Forbidden Road; sometimes on purpose, sometimes accidentally, but either way it usually doesn't end well for the traveler.

That's probably what happened to Father. He was a

courier, carrying messages and packages between star systems and planets and realms and cities and even points far in the past or a ways away in the far distant future. But he was also an explorer, hunting for unknown passageways. His greatest claim to fame — before he disappeared — was his discovery of three previously unmapped roads. He named one for my grandmother, one for himself, and one for my mother. The first two hardly get used at all: Grandmother's road leads to an ice planet in orbit around a dying red giant, while Father's leads to a swamp realm so vile that it took him a month to get the stink out of his skin.

Millicent Avenue, on the other hand — Mother's road — proved to be moderately lucrative. It leads to a pocket dimension: a single island in a vast blue sea warmed by a bright yellow sun. The weather is always perfect, the beaches are pink, and the sentient cetacean species that lives in that vast blue sea thinks that humans are cute.

Millicent Island: vacation paradise.

Father registered Millicent Avenue and, within a few years, the family was making a nice little income from the hoteliers who built resorts and bungalows, and tourists who made regular trips to the island.

Along with what Grandmother and Mother made on cab fare, it was enough to keep us going after he disappeared, until I was old enough to carry on the family legacy as a Walker.

And now here I am, about to repeat his disappearing act, as well, and it wasn't even my idea.

It's all Herbert's fault.

***

Herbert runs Myss Lyla's in Jerseea, a wild urban realm that exists entirely inside a hollowed out rock. No one knows if Jerseea is a planet within a larger universe, or if that's all there is; just the cave. No one has ever been able to tunnel all the way through the rock to find out.

And there is *lots* of tunneling going on throughout Jerseea. Mining is the city's primary source of income, and the whole thing is run by a handful of ultra-rich families who pay their workers just enough to survive and don't care about anything that doesn't impact their bottom line.

Like my regular deliveries of Hy-Brasil whiskey and Kitezh caviar.

(They do not go well together. Trust me on this.)

***

I stepped off Jerseea Avenue and onto the Crossroads. Other travelers faded in and out around me, coming and going; species of every description, loaded down with whatever they could carry. Someone bumped into me from behind, making the whiskey bottles clink, and another person jostled me from the side. There was growling and swearing.

I muttered a "Sorry," shifted my tall backpack, and exited the Crossroads as quickly as I could; which was not very quickly. Jerseea is always busy. No day or night here. Just blinding lights strung above the streets, a central clock set to a thirty hour cycle, and the distant walls and ceiling of the cave lost to the darkness.

And it was *loud*. Drills and diggers, engines and hammers, transports and railcars, music, shouting, talking, running. There was no such thing as *silence* in Jerseea. It was considered unnatural. It was a common belief that silence would drive a person mad. I had gotten tipsy once and tried to tell Herbert about the quiet little cove on Millicent Island where I liked to spend my limited free time: just me, the sand, and the sea. No wind, no crashing waves. Just quiet.

He had stared at me hard for a good minute, shaken his head sadly, and handed me a shot of Jerseean coffee (to "clear my head of that nonsense").

I pushed my way through the crowd, finding and joining a stream that was going in my general direction. The road was smooth beneath my boots, worn down by thousands of feet and tails over hundreds of years. Buildings leaned close on either side: apartments, brothels, restaurants, courier stations, grocery stores, bars, temples.

I paused long enough to toss a coin into the donation box for the temple of Mercurius, and then spit at the temple of Kryzkaltislk. (Mercurius likes money, Kryzkaltislk likes saliva. They're Gods. I don't have to understand them to curry their favor.)

I continued on, waving to Chinnis as they leaned out the front window of the Sleipnir Delivery Service. The logo of an eight-legged horse flickered above their head in gaudy red and gold. Chinnis waved three arms in return, one compound eyestalk pointed in my direction, the other two focused on their customer.

I slowed, frowning. Chinnis turned their full attention back to the customer. They were shaking all six arms now, eyestalks dancing. The customer appeared to be humanoid from my vantage point, but I couldn't be certain: long red cloak, the hood down, stubby black hair with electric red highlights; that was all I could see, and only for a moment.

The crowd closed around me again, the stream of species carrying me further into Jerseea.

By the time on the massive clocks that loomed over every street corner, it took me a good forty minutes to reach Myss Lyla's. The sign above the wide front doors glowed an inviting white and gold, drawing in customers in search of fine music, fine food, and even finer liquor. (Myss Lyla was about eight owners ago, and there was no one still around who could remember what she had looked like. Most people assumed that she had been the model for the smiling, buxom, four-armed blonde with the trays full of booze, but no one knew for certain.)

The doorman, gray-skinned and broad-shouldered, tipped his hat at my approach. "Fair welcome, one who is Walker Brown."

I smiled. "And fair travels to you, Peterrmenn. Boss still treating you right?"

Peterrmenn shrugged, his shoulders blocking one whole half of the doorway. "One cannot complain. Shall one guide you to the Herbert?"

"That would be splendid, thank you, Peterrmenn."

A slow nod and he turned, the doors parting. The smooth rock of the street was replaced by a thick carpet, beautifully patterned with soft whites and golds with black trim. The color scheme continued as the entryway opened up onto a dining room with cloth-covered tables, elegant servers, and a band and dance floor on the far side. The bar along the left wall was a streak of black, a sleek portrait of Myss Lyla hanging above it.

Peterrmenn and I barely got a glance as we crossed the room. The clientele were far too busy chatting, drinking, eating, and dancing. But Herbert spotted us.

He looked up from a row of colored bottles, grinned,

and waved us towards the near end of the bar. Filling a tray with drinks (some of them smoking, others on fire), he slid it towards one of the servers and then walked over to us.

"Thanks, Peterrmenn."

"The Herbert is welcome." Peterrmenn tipped his hat towards me again and turned away.

"Hold on," I called after him.

He stopped and I slid my backpack to the floor. It was more than half my height, the ridged sides mostly protecting the fragile contents. I untied the outer bag, flipped open the top lid, and pulled out a small clear flask. The chunky purple contents sloshed around inside as I held it out to Peterrmenn.

"As promised: one bottle of Oscirian berry wine."

His eyes lit up. The bottle was small in my hand; it was positively tiny in Peterrmenn's massive palm. "One offers deepest gratitude. One's mate will be most pleased."

"Any time. You need more, just let me know."

Peterrmenn grinned, showing quadruple rows of flat, hard teeth. He tucked the flask inside his jacket and headed back across the floor.

I turned to find Herbert glowering at me. "Thanks, Bertha. Much appreciated."

"For what?" I reached into the bag and started pulling out bottles of Hy-Brasil whiskey.

"*For what*, she says. Mating season for the Hemkirish, and you give him a bottle — an entire *bottle* — of their favorite aphrodisiac. I won't see him for a week."

"Good." I stacked the whiskey on the bar, two at a time. They disappeared almost as quickly, Herbert slipping them down behind the counter. "Not like Jerseea has labor laws. He needs the break, and some time with his mate. And you have plenty of other doormen."

"Not the point. He signed a contract, and, yes, I have plenty of other doormen, but he's the best. Big, polite, never loses his temper. Big."

I shrugged and started unloading the canisters of Kitezh caviar onto the bar.

"Have any problems?" he asked.

"Nah." I shook my head. "Though I might have issues with your order of acorns from Pohjola. Rumor has it that Louhi is on the warpath again and might close off the road."

Herbert paused, a handful of canisters still on the bartop. "Are you saying you may not be able to fulfill your contract?"

I stood and pressed my hands to the edge of the counter, leaning towards him. I spoke very carefully. "I am saying that a Witch-Goddess closing off her realm is outside my control and that, as the Walker, I have final say in whether or not a realm is too dangerous to visit or a road too dangerous to travel. Per said contract, you may request a substitution if I cannot acquire Pohjolan acorns."

I smiled.

He scowled.

I held out my hand. "As you have accepted delivery, payment please."

***

I was hungry, so I stuck around to eat. Myss Lyla's really does have excellent food and, as an outside contractor, I was entitled to a twenty-five percent discount. Herbert got back five of his coins, and I got a spiced beef and apricot salad, garlic cheese bread, and a Hemkirish chocolate mousse for dessert.

Win-win.

I pulled up a stool and planted myself at the end of the bar, my backpack tucked against my legs. I ate slowly, reveling in the chance to just sit for a while after having been on the roads for so long. (How much time had passed back in Detroit? A month?) Various species twirled around the dance floor, most of them humanoid at the moment, which meant that the band was playing palatable music.

I was licking my spoon and handing my clean plates back to a server when I spotted Herbert at the far end of the bar. He was leaning over the counter, speaking with someone that I couldn't see. Then the crowd of patrons and servers shifted.

Red cloak with the hood down, stubby black hair with electric red highlights, humanoid.

The customer from Sleipnir Delivery Services.

At least, I was fairly sure.

Herbert half-turned, tilting his head in my direction. I held his gaze, lifting my eyebrows in a *Yes, what's up?* expression. He turned away, motioning to Red Cloak with his hand. More conversation. The crowd around the bar shifted again and I lost sight of Red Cloak.

Tossing my spoon into the dirty dishes bin behind the counter, I bent to pick up my bag — only to find Red Cloak standing right next to me.

Herbert stepped around from behind the bar, waving a hand between us. "Bertha Brown, may I extend fair introductions to Amkhira. Amkhira, may I extend fair introductions to Bertha Brown, a fifth generation Walker."

Amkhira. Just Amkhira. No occupation, no home-realm or homeworld, no guild or temple affiliation.

Humanoid. Very pale, almost icy blue eyes. Skin that was several shades darker than their hair. The electric red highlights in their hair continued as flashing tattoos that shifted and slid across their face, changing shape. The cloak was closed tight, preventing me from seeing anything below their neck.

"Fair travels to you, Amkhira."

"And to you, Walker Brown." Their voice was rough, grating, like rocks scratching.

"Amkhira has need of a Walker's services." Herbert smiled at me. "They learned of you from Chinnis and, after hearing their problem, I agree that you are the best Walker for the job. Even better, I can call in my substitution."

I scowled at him. "I haven't taken the job yet."

"But you will."

A server popped up next to me, holding a stool. He set it down and Amkhira carefully slid into place, cloak still closed tight. Jaw clenched, I settled back on my own seat.

"Consider Amkhira's proposal carefully. And, when you accept, I in turn will accept no fewer than three whole egg shells from Zerzurrah. One as a substitute for the Pohjolan acorns, and two at my own expense."

I blinked. "What?"

Amkhira's voice made my teeth grit. "You are welcome beyond the gates of that city. You may travel the road to Zerzurrah without fear of being turned away."

I shifted on the stool. "*Once.* I have a one-time pass. And I was —" I shot Herbert an irritated glare "— saving it."

Amkhira's cloak ruffled as something moved beneath it. Their hand emerged, or something approximating a hand: the fingers and palm were cracked an even darker black than their face and hair. No electric red tattoos here.

In the center of their hand lay a tiny cetacean, delicately carved from pink stone. It was so expertly done that, for a moment, I thought it was a real dolphin.

I stared at the sculpture, my heart thudding. "Where did you get that?"

"Your father carved this for me, as proof of the truth of my words." Amkhira's gaze was unblinking. "I require an item from within the walls of Zerzurrah. Acquire it for me, and I will guide you to your father."

~ TWO ~

REMEMBER WHEN I SAID THAT FATHER WAS RECOGNIZED FOR mapping three previously unknown roads? Well, I found one, too.

It was a complete accident. We were traveling home along Khendaar Lane, a little-used path between Detroit and the desert realm of Khendaar; the scenic route, Father liked to call it.

And I ... wandered away.

I was eight years old. Call it undeveloped, untrained Walker instincts. I knew there was a road, so I took it.

What I had found was a back door into Zerzurrah, a twisty, weedy little pathway that probably hadn't been walked since the Gods created that realm eons ago. Instead of coming up the main road and stopping at the gate — where the Zerzurrahns ran an invitation-only auction a few days every year — I popped out in the middle of the hatchery.

The Zerzurrahns freaked.

Every species has their own creation myth, and Zerzur-rahns are no exception. They consider themselves to be the first, best, and truest children of the Gods. Given the fact that they're borderline immortal, their blood will cure almost any illness, and their feathers are known to regenerate dead ecosystems, they might be right.

Which, of course, also makes them prime targets for hunters, mercenaries, mad scientists, soulless corporations, and really really rich people.

When the Zerzurrahns realized what I had discovered, they didn't kill me. Maybe it was my family's reputation; maybe it was their past dealings with my family; maybe they just couldn't kill a child. Instead, they made a hasty offer: leave the road unregistered, and I would be granted a full-access pass to their city. I could go anywhere. See anything. Buy anything.

Once.

Father was a good man. He knew that registering that back road — making it public knowledge — was tantamount to genocide. The Zerzurrahns would never be able to keep out everyone who wanted to kill them, experiment on them, and harvest them for parts.

I agreed. Father put the word out that I had a city pass, though he never, ever explained how I had acquired it. (Rumors were plentiful and wild.) People from worlds we had never even heard of reached out to him with their shopping lists. Money poured in. Other people tried to buy my pass off him, promising even more money. He just laughed.

And a month later, Father disappeared.

Had he been killed for access to Zerzurrah? Or was his disappearance just a tragic accident? Had he found a Forbidden Road? Gotten lost and wandered away?

We didn't know. Grandmother, Mother, and I had eventually resigned ourselves to the fact that we would likely never know.

And my city pass? I never used it. Holding onto it for a rainy day seemed like a good idea. Grandmother insisted, even after we had to return all of the money that had been sent by those eager shoppers; the income from Millicent Avenue and their taxi cabs was just enough to keep us going until I finished my apprenticeship and took over Father's business.

People still try to buy my pass. Several of Jerseea's wealthy families had tried on more than one occasion; so had the Sayahk of Khendaar, the Elders of Homana, and the Frtilsk of Frtilsk.

But Amkhira had the one thing that I would absolutely, without question sacrifice that pass to find: my Father.

***

"How?" I stammered.

Amkhira blinked at me slowly, and remained silent. The pink carved cetacean disappeared back beneath their cloak.

Herbert cleared his throat. "I believe that Walker Brown is attempting to ask how you would like to go about making arrangements for your journey —"

"Oh that is *not* what I'm asking and you know it!" I punched his shoulder. Turning back to Amkhira, I leaned closer. "*How* did you find him? I looked for *years*."

"I will not say. Just as you will not say how you acquired safe passage to Zerzurrah."

I felt my jaw clench. My chest was tight, and my heart was beating too fast. "Fine. The contract is as follows: I will enter Zerzurrah and acquire ... what is it exactly that you need?"

"A page from a book. The original, not a copy." Amkhira tilted their head slightly, taking in our crowded surroundings. "I will specify the book later."

"Very well. I will enter Zerzurrah and acquire an unspecified page from an as-yet unspecified book, which you will pay for ...?"

This time, Amkhira looked around. Apparently satisfied, their hand emerged again, this time holding a small piece of folded cloth. Amkhira held it towards me.

I took it carefully. The cloth was fine and light in my hands, doing little to hide the shape and color of the object wrapped inside it. My breath caught. I felt Herbert edge closer as I gently unfolded the fabric.

Amber. A tiny, perfect tear-shaped bead, the spark of light within setting off the dark golden hue.

This was not regular amber, the kind that could be found on the shores of innumerable oceans. No, this was divine amber, the crystalized tears shed by Freyja as she wandered the worlds in search of her husband.

The Zerzurrahns had a corner on the market. They bought every amber tear that became available. Rumor had it that they had a private company of Walkers whose only job was to hunt down divine amber. My great-great-grandmother had launched the family courier service with the money earned by selling the Zerzurrahns the single tear she had found by accident.

They were mad for the stuff, and no one knew why.

I swallowed. "That should do it. And, in exchange for acquiring a page from a book, you will safely guide me to my Father, and then allow us to safely return home to Detroit."

Amkhira blinked slowly, silent. Then an equally slow nod. "Agreed."

Herbert clapped his hands together. "Excellent! As I said, Bertha, three whole egg shells." A bag of coins plopped into my lap. "And I cannot emphasize enough: *whole* egg shells. Would you like me to have Peterrmenn escort you to the Crossroads? He is very good at clearing a path."

"No, I would —" I drew a breath. Between the servers, the bouncers, the musicians, and the guests, it would not be long before word got out that I was loaded down with coins and an amber tear, *and* that I was on my way to Zerzurrah. Ambush followed quickly by death was a definite possibility. Actually, I wouldn't be surprised if Jerseea's ruling families intercepted me en route to the Crossroads and made me an offer I shouldn't refuse. "Yes. Fine." I stood, shoved the coin pouch and the cloth-wrapped amber tear inside my shirt, and grabbed my bag.

Amkhira stood, as well. "I will accompany you. You return to your home realm, yes?"

"That's the plan."

No response.

I could only wonder how Grandmother and Mother would react when Amkhira walked through the front door.

***

Peterrmenn wasn't just very good at clearing a path. He was excellent. Everything got out of his way, even the transport buses and the heavy cargo carriers.

As we neared Sleipnir Delivery Service, Chinnis swept an eyestalk back and forth. A sort-of apology with a question mark on the end.

I waggled three fingers in response, accepting the sort-of apology, but refusing to stop and explain any further.

(I slowed down enough to toss another handful of coins

into the offering box in front of Mercurius' temple, though. Just to be safe.)

Amkhira followed along behind me. I couldn't hear their footsteps over the shouting, grinding, and roaring, but they just seemed to ... well, almost glide over the road. There wasn't so much as a flutter of movement beneath their cloak. Actually, I wasn't even sure if they were breathing.

When we reached the Crossroads, Peterrmenn turned and looked down at me, frowning. "Fair travels, Walker Brown. Do not become deceased. This one enjoys seeing you and engaging in stimulating conversation."

I smiled up at him and gently tapped a fist against his arm; it was wider around than my thigh. "Right back at you. And you enjoy that Oscirian berry wine."

A solemn nod, and he backed away a few steps until he was clear of the Crossroads. Around us, other Walkers moved in a chaotic knot, coming and going, popping in and out of Jerseea, following one road or another, loaded down with supplies and trade goods and letters.

I held out my hand to Amkhira. "Shall we?"

They glanced down, blinked slowly, then looked back up. That strange, dark, cracked approximation of a hand emerged from their cloak to close around mine; stubby, rough fingers and a scratchy palm. I felt very faint sparks against my skin.

It was unnerving.

Keeping my expression neutral, I drew a deep breath, and envisioned the road that I wanted to travel and my destination. Exhaling long and slow, I whispered the name of the road, tightened my grip on Amkhira's hand, and stepped forward.

***

Detroit Boulevard is wide and always busy. I could vaguely see and hear the hordes of Walkers around us: they were smears of deep purple and red in an infinite brightness, exhalations and whispers a wind that pulled at my clothes and pushed against my ears.

Amkhira was more substantial, and strangely so: black instead of purple or red, an unexpected weight on my arm, and ... singing?

They were no longer silent. That grating, gravelly voice had transformed into a warm hum; like a hummingbird or a bumble bee. It danced across my skin, thrumming, raising the hairs on the back of my neck. Electricity moved across my flesh along with the hum. A shiver slid down my spine, and the amber tear felt warm against my chest.

I stumbled in surprise, but quickly caught myself. If my concentration broke, we would be lost.

I focused on the road, solid beneath my feet. Here, only the road was real, tangible. *Only* the road was supposed to be tangible. I wiggled my fingers against the strange almost-solidness of Amkhira's hand, their humming song rising and falling.

Forward, step by step, through the brightness, through the throng. I continued to exhale, my breath and voice joining those of all the Walkers around me; perhaps even the echo of the Gods who had first walked these roads into existence.

Forward, step by step.

Amkhira felt heavier.

My lungs tightened, my breath nearly gone, my whisper beginning to fade.

Heavier, dragging on my arm, my shoulder.

Forward.

And then we were at the Crossroads of Detroit. The infinite brightness was gone, replaced by the cool sun of a spring day. The wind and echoing whispers of the other Walkers was replaced by a breeze that smelled of asphalt, diesel, and rubber, and that carried the sounds of tires and horns.

I gasped, dropping Amkhira's hand, and sucked fresh air into my lungs.

Traveling alone was relatively easy. Having to drag along a non-Walker was another matter entirely; I could usually carry one, maybe two other people; but none had ever felt like Amkhira.

"You are weak. Your father did not experience such difficulties."

Hands braced on my knees, bag pressing down on my back, I glared up at Amkhira. "Yes, you're right. My father is a stronger Walker. But *I* have the pass into Zerzurrah." I straightened, waiting. I dug my single-number pager out of an interior pocket, hit the call button, and shoved it back into my pocket, still waiting.

No apology was forthcoming. Amkhira just blinked at me, eyes slowly closing and opening.

"Right." Shifting the backpack into a more comfortable position, I led the way through the Crossroads and towards Detroit proper.

Thousands of Walkers swirled around us, coming and going. A Hemkirish carrying a massive boulder of Muspelheim obsidian. A deer-like Cervithian, antlers strung with beads and ribbons, flanks covered in bulging packages. A swarm of tiny Pixins zipped past my head, each carrying a message scroll bound at their waists. Humans and Neanderthals, Oscirians and Felinians, Drakes and Foxin. And, looming beyond and above us all, the skyline of Detroit: sharp steel and gleaming glass skyscrapers, massive graceful statues of concrete and marble, cable cars and elevated trains and dirigibles. Straight ahead, straddling the Northern Gate of the Crossroads, stood a marble likeness of Cadillaq himself; instinct had led him here, to the nexus point where one hundred and thirteen roads intersected; business savvy led him to give up Walking and found a city.

Jerseea was an important realm thanks to its mining operation, but its Crossroads was the nexus for only nineteen roads. It would never become a trade and diplomatic hub as important as Detroit — something which, I am sure, endlessly aggravated the city's ruling families.

It took us an hour to navigate through the crowds. Ten minutes into our trek, I felt the pager vibrate. Smiling, I quickened my steps. Beyond the gate, trucks and transports and cabs fought for the few hundred parking slots or circled slowly, belching exhaust even as they were unloaded and reloaded with goods from a hundred worlds and realms and eras.

I pushed my way around a truck that reeked of old fish and clams. Straining, I lifted onto my toes, scanning the swarm of vehicles. After long minutes, I spotted a familiar cab, its bright yellow paint and chrome hood ornament gleaming in the sun.

Stepping forward, I whistled loudly, raising my hand.

The driver saw me through the window. Grinning and waving, she accelerated and twisted the cab, expertly weaving through the other vehicles until she could pull up next to me. She leapt out, her fat black braids swinging under her grey tweed cap as she dashed around her car and wrapped me in a tight hug. She didn't care how it wrinkled her uniform; she never did. "Bertha, my precious girl! Welcome home! Welcome home!"

"Hello, Mother." I returned the hug and the grin, inhaling the comforting scents of leather and wood and bergamot. "How long have I been gone?"

One last tight grip and she leaned away, her fingers still wrapped around my arms. "Forty-two days. Have any problems in Kitezh?"

"Nope. But Louhi might be shutting the road to Pohjola."

Mother scowled, tugging on the hem of her dark grey jacket. "Again? One of her daughters run off again?"

I shrugged. "Probably." I cleared my throat. "This is Amkhira. Something's come up. Is Grandmother still on shift?"

Mother pulled a shiny silver fob watch from her pocket and snapped open the lid; the chain clinked softly. "She should just be getting off now." Mother looked up as she tucked the watch away again, her gaze darting between me and Amkhira. "Can you talk about it here?"

I shook my head.

"In that case, let's head home." She quirked an eyebrow at Amkhira. "Is there someplace I can take you?"

I cleared my throat again. "Yeah. Home."

***

It was quiet inside the cab. Mother kept the radio turned down, the music a soft background to the shush of the tires and the rumble of the engine.

The interior of the cab was as pristine as always: soft leather seats, spotless carpet and windows, wooden trim and dashboard. I was almost afraid to touch anything.

Detroit hadn't changed, either. Dark asphalt streets with bright yellow stripes, sidewalks so white that it almost hurt to look at them, shimmering glass and steel buildings; here and there, carefully sculpted and maintained trees and flowers, their dead leaves and petals swept up almost as soon as they fell.

But then I had only been gone forty-two days. Detroit had been around for almost a thousand years, and even after all this time, Cadillaq would have no trouble recognizing the skyline.

Mother pulled into the reserved parking slot just half a block down from our apartment building. One of the perks of being a cab driver: guaranteed parking paid for by the company.

As soon as I climbed out, she wrapped an arm around my shoulders, hugging me close. We tripped down the sidewalk together, just enjoying one another's touch again after being separated for so long.

I couldn't hear Amkhira behind us, but I caught their distorted reflection in windows and steel support beams.

Branson tipped his hat as we approached the front doors. His white gloves were spotless, and the brass buttons on his long jacket shone in the sun. "Welcome home, Ms. Brown. Fun trip?"

"As always, Branson, as always. Anything to report?"

Mother rolled her eyes.

"Mr. Hogarth's schnauzer had her puppies. Two of the dryers are still on the fritz. A colony of Mousekinth have moved into 13-D and are refusing to pay rent in any recognized coinage. And the city's entire baseball team defected to Londinium."

I wrinkled my nose in sympathy. "I'm sorry you won't be able to watch the playoffs this year."

Branson shrugged and reached for the shiny door handle. "Ah, well. Not like they've gotten to the finals in my lifetime, or ever will."

"Ugh. Enough." Mother tugged me through the door and into the cool entryway. "This girl needs to get off her feet."

Branson chuckled and tipped his hat again. "Yes, ma'am."

I looked up at Mother. "Dare I ask what the Mousekinth are using as coinage?"

"The bodies of their fallen warriors."

"Ick?"

We crossed the entryway, passing the crowded wall of public shrines: Ganesh and Lakshmi, Hermes and Iris, Hekate, Kryzkaltislk and Phfarzakk, Abeona and Adiona, Mercurius, Odhinn and Sleipnir, Yacatecuhtli, Shanxxix and Horxxix. Curls of incense rose above the altars, which were weighed down with flowers, coins, feathers, glass eyes, ribbons, miniature maps, and colorful stones.

Mother tapped the call button for the elevator. "According to Mr. Hogarth, who can hear it all through his walls, the Mousekinth hold gladiatorial battles every day. *Every day.* The fallen warriors are stripped to their bones, which are then laid out in the hallway as payment." Mother's nose wrinkled. "His schnauzer ate one. Didn't know what it was. The Mousekinth were *not* happy. Threatened to eat her puppies in retaliation."

The elevator pinged and the doors soundlessly slipped open.

"Soooo ... they're being evicted?"

Mother followed me in, tugging off her hat to tuck it under her arm. "Landlord's trying, but the Mousekinth have a *really* good lawyer."

Amkhira trailed along silently. Still not a ripple under the red cloak. They looked between us as the doors slid shut.

"This is a nonsensical conversation."

"It is a completely sensical conversation," I countered and hit the button for the twentieth floor.

Gears rumbled, and up we went.

"We must depart for Zerzurrah as soon as possible."

Mother's head snapped around, her braids flying. "What?"

"The sooner I acquire the map, the sooner your mate and father will be returned to you."

Mother's mouth fell open and she gaped at Amkhira. "I — what? Bertha?" She turned to me, eyes wide. She had paled noticeably and she gripped her hat so tightly that she had crushed the brim.

"I, um, yeah. They say they know where Father is. They want to trade. Apparently for a Zerzurrahn map. Map of what? Mom!"

Mother dropped back against the wall, her legs quivering. She grabbed my hand, squeezing painfully. "Your Father — Jeremiah? He — he's alive? He —" She was crying now. She slid to the floor, dragging me down with her. "I always thought — I hoped — I —" She sucked in a deep breath. Her whole body was shaking. When she spoke again, her voice was a thin whisper. "He's coming home?"

I glanced up at Amkhira. "Yes. If they're telling the truth —"

"I do not deceive you, Walker Brown."

"Then Father's coming home."

A sob erupted from Mother's chest, a horrible sound of grief and hope. She wrapped her arms around me, burying her face in my chest. I crouched awkwardly, half my weight on my big backpack, my arms wrapped around her, too. It took me a moment to realize that I was crying, as well, my nose running, my throat raw.

The elevator pinged and the doors slid open.

Amkhira watched us, silent and unblinking.

***

That was how Grandmother found us. She must have heard the elevator doors open. She came running down the hallway, still in her cabbie uniform, but she had swapped out her shiny boots for comfy bunny slippers.

She slid to a halt on the carpet, almost falling. "Millicent? Bertha, are you okay? Are you hurt? What in Hermes' name is going on?"

Mother was hiccuping and sobbing so hard that she could barely speak. "Jeremiah. J-J-Jeremiah. He's coming home."

Grandmother raised a trembling hand to cover her mouth. Her eyes bulged and she blinked rapidly. "My boy? My boy?" Her voice shook.

Then she swallowed hard. Shaking her head, she dropped her hand and reached for Mother. "Come on now. Off the floor. Let's get you both inside." Grandmother dropped a quick head tilt towards Amkhira. "Sorry for holding you up."

"They're with us." I shoved my shoulder under Mother's arm and helped her down the hallway. I pushed through the unlocked door and gently lowered her onto the couch.

Mother shook her head as I did so, pressing one hand into the soft cushions. "No. I'm okay. I'll be okay. Just — very sudden."

Dumping my bag in a chair, I headed into the kitchen to pour a glass of water. Behind me, I could hear Grandmother locking the door and snapping questions.

"What do you mean Jeremiah is coming home? Bertha, what is going on? Who is this person?"

When I returned to the living room, she took the glass from me, handed it to Mother, and pointed at the chair. "Sit. Explain."

"There is little to explain." Amkhira's voice grated, rock grinding. They almost sounded angry, frustrated. "Walker Brown shall purchase a page from the *Infinite Atlas* —"

Mother choked on her water.

"— and in exchange I shall lead her to her father. It is a straightforward transaction. I do not understand this need for repeated explanations or for emotional displays. These delays are unnecessary. We must depart."

"Absolutely not," Grandmother snapped. Her hand settled on my shoulder. "I want my son back, probably more than you can possibly imagine. But Bertha has been traveling for over a month. She needs to rest. One day." She looked down at me for confirmation. "One day."

Amkhira was silent. They stared at Grandmother for a long moment, electric tattoos churning over their forehead and cheeks. The tattoos gradually slowed and then stilled. Amkhira turned their back to us and glided over to the window. They remained there, unmoving; definitely not breathing.

Mother drained her glass, stood, and tilted her chin towards the kitchen. Grandmother and I followed. Mother pulled us into a tight circle along the back counter and flipped on the radio. Aretha Franklin's clarion voice filled the apartment.

Mother leaned in, arms crossed. "The *Infinite Atlas*?" she hissed.

"I didn't know! They just said a page from a book. In Zerzurrah. I had no idea that's where the *Atlas* was!"

Grandmother snorted. "I don't think anyone is supposed to know where it is."

"So how do *they* know?" Mother flicked a finger towards Amkhira, invisible beyond the kitchen wall.

I shrugged helplessly.

Mother sighed and rubbed a hand over the back of her neck. "Are you absolutely *sure* that they know where Jeremiah is?"

"They said as much, and in front of Herbert. He witnessed the transaction, and we shook on it."

Grandmother "hhmed," her lips thin.

Before I could continue, a loud beep-buzz momentarily drowned out Aretha.

Mother grumbled and returned to the living room. Grandmother and I trailed after her, pausing in the doorway of the kitchen. She pressed the button on the call box beside the front door. "Yes, Branson?"

"Sorry, Mrs. Brown, but I have some gentlemen here who would like to speak with Walker Brown. Has she returned home yet?"

Mother's head pulled back. She shot a quick glance at me. "No, I'm sorry, we haven't —"

There was a startled grunt, a cry of pain, and a long beeeeeeep as something was rammed into the entryway call box. Mother released the button, stumbling back a step.

Then silence.

"Okay." Grandmother kicked off her bunny slippers, grabbed my bag off the chair, and threw it at me. I caught it and swung it over my back. "Time to go. Whoever they are, they'll be coming up the elevator and probably up the stairs, too." She unlocked and yanked open the door. "Go out the back way."

I opened my mouth to protest, then closed it. I could hear the distant rumble of the elevator.

I wrapped my arms tight around Grandmother. Mother hugged me from behind. I inhaled, trying to hold onto the sensation of being surrounded by their warmth and love.

Too soon, we all let go.

"Come on, Amkhira." I bolted out the door, not bothering to look behind me to see if they were following.

At the far end of the hall, I slowed and quietly pushed open the door to the stairwell. Behind me, I could hear the elevator drawing closer. Below, muffled shouts and racing footsteps coming up, up, up.

Stepping inside, I waved for Amkhira to pass me, then just as carefully closed the door. Finger to my lips, I motioned down.

And down we went.

I hugged the wall, lifting and dropping my feet as quietly as possible. Amkhira floated along behind me. I was beginning to wonder if they even *had* feet. Or legs.

The voices and footsteps from below were getting louder, closer.

I stumbled, catching myself against the wall. Pushed back up and kept going, down, down, down.

And almost ran right into Aselolla. She lifted all four of her arms and grinned, skin and long hair shifting from the yellow of shock to the deep blue of delight.

"Bertha!" she squealed. "I didn't know you were home! How wondrous!"

"Uh."

The shouts from below got louder, the footsteps speeding up.

"Sorry, Aselolla!" I pushed around her, leaning over the railing, and caught a glimpse of figures running up the stairs. One of the figures paused to glare up at me: humanoid, bald, bulky, black business suit. He lifted an arm towards me and I leapt back from the railing, jumping down two, three, five steps. "I explain everything later!" I yelled, and shoved open the door to the thirteenth floor.

Aselolla's delighted farewell followed me, bouncing off the walls. "Okay, Bertha! Have a good day!"

Down the hall. 13-K, 13-J, 13-I. Around the corner.

I was yelling now. "Mr. Hogarth! Mr. Hogarth!"

Wild yipping answered me from far end of the hall.

Fire hose.

I skidded to a halt, turned, and ripped open the fire hose cabinet. Unspooling the hose, I snapped to Amkhira, "Turn it on!" and yelled again, "Mr. Hogarth!"

From the corner of my eye, I saw the door to 13-A swing open. Mr. Hogarth stuck his head out into the hallway, frowning, yipping schnauzer under one arm. A couple of puppies tumbled around his ankles.

Bones crunched under my feet.

I lifted my leg and kicked at the door of 13-D. It rattled in the frame. Another kick.

"Bertha! What in Cerberus' na —"

A third kick. The wood cracked. The schnauzer was still yipping and the puppies had joined in. I thought I heard squeaking from inside the apartment. A lot of squeaking.

Fourth, and the door crashed open.

No furniture, no curtains. Sunlight flooded the room from the large sliding glass doors along the back wall. The Mousekinth had ripped up the carpet to create nests that towered over my head. They had chewed into the drywall, creating openings that mimicked the soaring apartment building itself. The bare wooden floor — what I could see of it — was covered in ritualistic diagrams and bones. So many bones.

The Mousekinth stared at me. Hundreds of them. No, thousands. From the floor, from the carpet nests, from the holes in the walls, from the ceiling fan and the door ledge. Their white fur and their long tails were painted in gaudy reds and greens, and they carried knives and spears fashioned from aluminum cans and paperclips and chips of colored glass.

As one, they opened their mouths and bared their sharp mousey teeth.

I heard the door to the stairwell crash open. Loud steps pounding down the hallway.

"Death to Mousekinth!" I screamed and flipped on the hose.

Water surged through the fabric and out the nozzle. The Mousekinth shrieked at the sudden rainstorm.

I dropped the hose, sending the water roiling across the wooden floor, carrying bones and other debris, wiping away the ritual diagrams. I bolted the rest of the way down the corridor, shouting a hurried apology to Mr. Hogarth as I shoved my way into his apartment. Amkhira glided in silently behind me. The puppies floundered around my feet, and I had to lift my boots carefully to step around them.

Mr. Hogarth followed me, still stuttering confused questions. The schnauzer was still yipping.

There were screams from the hallway, and shouts of bafflement, and then pain and terror.

I stopped, turned, took a very quick peek.

The dozen black business suits, whoever they were, had

made it no further than 13-D. The Mousekinth swarmed out of the apartment, around the roiling water, along the walls and even the ceiling. The bulky, balding human in the lead clutched and tore at his clothes, ripping away the Mousekinth who were stabbing and biting him. Blood dribbled from his hands, his cheeks, the top of his head. More Mousekinth dropped from the ceiling, clinging to his ears and eyelids, biting.

He screamed, flailing, the men behind him doing the same.

I slammed the door shut.

"Might want to keep that locked, thanks Mr. Hogarth, I'll explain everything later, sorry!"

Across the living room, around the mess of dog toys and the mass shrine to Anubis, Wepwawet, Cerberus, and Hades, to the sliding glass doors. I slapped one open and stepped out onto the very narrow patio.

Our building was twenty-seven stories. The building to the east — directly across from Mr. Hogarth's apartment — was only thirteen stories high.

It had been something of a game while I was growing up. The kids in my building (me, Aselolla, Judith and Judy, Shiranthz) would plot out routes from our roof, down, and across as many rooftops as we could, going as far as we could without touching the ground. The only way out of our building was the back way: from a deck on the thirteenth floor.

It had driven Mother crazy. Father had called it good Walker training; he had done the same growing up.

I could still hear screams in the hallway. Further away, sirens, coming from the street and from a dirigible. I caught the flash of lights in the corner of my eye, high up in the sky.

The alley swelled below me, a cavern of steel, concrete, and glass.

Eight feet.

I could do this. I had done this before. I could do it again.

Backing up into Mr. Hogarth's apartment again, I drew a deep breath. Amkhira watched me silently, hovering just outside. The electric sparks in their stubby hair reflected in the glass of the door. Mr. Hogarth stared at me, his eyes wide, his arms filled with wriggling puppies.

I ran. My bag bounced against my back. I jumped, one foot hitting the top of the railing. I pushed off, arms swinging, legs kicking. I flew.

I landed hard. Gravel skidded beneath my boots. My arms flailed as I struggled for balance. Heat and light radiated off the roof, making me squint.

Panting, I straightened. And found Amkhira beside me, cloak rustling softly in the breeze.

"We depart now for Zerzurrah, yes?" they asked. Aggravation tinged the question.

I didn't bother to answer. I could hear shouts and pounding coming from Mr. Hogarth's apartment. Casting up a quick prayer to his favored Gods that he and the puppies would be safe, I turned and raced across the roof, across Detroit, towards the Crossroads, and my father.

~ THREE ~

It took us three hours to reach the Crossroads. We stuck to buildings: rooftops, fire escapes, hallways, in and out through windows. We stayed under cover as much as possible, and off the street. We got plenty of weird looks, but just as many people completely ignored us; too busy going about their own business.

We finally ran out of buildings and had to stop.

We huddled in a fourth floor stairwell, peering out the narrow window. The vast parking lot and wheel of circling vehicles spread out in front of us, then the arch of the Eastern Gate, and the Crossroads at the center. There was no statue of Cadillaq here, as there was at the Northern Gate; instead, the archway itself was decorated with the likenesses and iconography of dozens of Deities. Masses of beings popped in and out of Detroit's nexus, only spots of moving color from this distance. Vehicles chugged and whirred and whined, horns honking, brakes squeaking, people yelling and gesturing.

A woman snarling into a phone had barely given us a glance when we climbed off the fire escape and through her window. I had never been in this building before, but, according to the listings beside the elevator, the eight story white stone and steel structure was mostly offices and apartments, with an import/export business on the ground floor.

I mentally scrambled through one plan after another as I continued to watch the Crossroads. Beside me, Amkhira floated silently, but I could feel their agitation and impatience. It was definitely beginning to grate on me.

Maybe we could hide in a box? Find one that was being shipped out?

No, that was stupid.

Steal a couple of uniforms?

I flicked a glance at Amkhira from the corner of my eye.

Maybe. That might be doable.

I couldn't be certain, but I was fairly sure that the hostile business suits worked for one of Jerseea's families; maybe more than one. Our trip from Myss Lyla's through Jerseea and home had been quick. There was almost no chance that word had spread to other realms about my upcoming trip to Zerzurrah.

Other than "people in business suits covered in Mousekinth bites" I had no idea who to watch for, who to avoid. There could be one person out there waiting for us, or a hundred.

And the suits were hostile. Branson had good instincts; that's what made him such a highly sought-after front door man. He'd stopped them at the door and warned us, and they had hurt him. That awful sound had probably been his face being smashed into the call box.

I hoped that he was okay.

I hoped that Mother and Grandmother were okay, and Mr. Hogarth and his puppies.

Please let them all be okay.

I drew a deep breath, steadying my thoughts.

"We leave soon, yes?" Amkhira asked, voice like rocks shattering and rolling over gravel.

"Yep. Just plotting."

We only needed to get safely through the traffic. We just had to cross through one of the gates, into the nexus proper. I was a strong enough Walker that I didn't need to be near the center; even from the edge, I could find the road I needed.

Nothing fancy. We needed to get to Zerzurrah as quickly as possible. Only fifty roads connected to Zerzurrah Avenue. From here, that meant a hop from Detroit down Brysbyland Lane to the Brysbyland Crossroads, then Feitha Avenue to the Feitha Crossroads, and straight up Zerzurrah Avenue.

The gate outside of Zerzurrah would be mostly empty right now. No market had been announced, but there were always idiots hoping to talk or buy their way in; professional shoppers, too, sitting in their booths and only too happy to take someone else's wish list and money and wait for market day.

I doubted that any of them would recognize me, but the doors opening for me would certainly cause a reaction.

"You think too long. I will take you."

"What?" I frowned at Amkhira.

"I can carry you to the edge of the nexus."

"How?"

"I —" A long pause, Amkhira's dark face wrinkling. Their skin seemed to crack, showing red beneath, and then smoothed over. "I do not know the words. I am here, and I reach out, stretch, then I am there. But no further than the edge of the nexus. I cannot proceed without you — without a Walker."

"Okaaay. Okay." Intra-world walking of some sort? I had never heard of such a thing, but it explained Amkhira's ability to suddenly *appear*.

Of course, we could have saved ourselves three hours of dodging from building to building if Amkhira had mentioned their ability earlier.

I suppressed another sigh and nodded. "You get us to the gate, and I'll take it from there."

I held out my hand. Amkhira stared at me. Their cloak rustled and their own approximation of a hand emerged, still dark and cracked; *mostly* cracked; the palm and the undersides of several of their fingers looked slightly melted, as did the area around their wrist. I couldn't see anything beyond that.

Their fingers made grinding sounds as they closed around my sleeve.

"So is th —"

The roads between realities are brilliant white and light and wind and slow, deliberate steps. This was ... not. This was every color I had ever seen and a thousand more that I couldn't name, let alone imagine. It was a silence so profound that I could hear my own cells dividing and my synapses firing sparks of electricity. It was moving in every direction simultaneously without moving.

And then it stopped.

Someone was screaming.

I was screaming.

I collapsed, boneless, face cracking against the concrete. Sound assaulted me from every side. My lungs wouldn't work. My muscles spasmed.

"Walker Brown. Walker Brown, you must arise."

I think I made a sound. I tasted blood. My hands twitched. I shifted my shoulders and managed to get my arms under my torso. The top of my backpack banged into my head.

"Walker Brown." Amkhira was past aggravated now. They sounded truly pissed, their voice a violent rumble.

I grunted. My whole face felt hot. "Yep." That was blood in my mouth. I could feel it rolling down my throat. I must have broken my nose when I hit the concrete. "Wat waz zhat?"

No answer.

I pushed against the ground, my arms shaking. My legs were next, spasms gradually fading enough that I could maneuver my knees into position. I shoved back, wobbled, and managed to sit upright.

Nasty red sparks tore through Amkhira's hair, racing down their neck to disappear beneath their cloak. And their cloak was twisting and heaving.

Yep. Amkhira was definitely pissed.

"Little wharning nesht time," I slurred, and spat a wad of blood.

The Eastern Gate loomed above us, a silvery archway. Deities looked down at us with expressions ranging from benevolent to curious to tolerant, their likenesses carved into the glimmering silver. Walkers loaded down with cargo or trailing passengers streamed around us, clogging the archway. Someone bumped into my backpack, and didn't even pause to apologize.

I pulled my sleeve down over my hand and wiped it across my face. It came back streaked red.

Legs still uncertain, I half-stood, wobbled, and straightened.

Amkhira floated a short distance away, angry red sparks still dancing across their cheeks and through their hair.

So many questions.

No time for questions.

I pulled my pager out of its pocket, looking around as I did so. I dialed the single number stored in its memory, moving towards a gleaming trash can. I waited for confirmation that it had connected. The pager vibrated. If Mother and Grandmother were safe, they would know that I had reached the Crossroads and was on my way. I ripped off the back cover, tore out the battery, and tossed the separate pieces into the trash.

I spit another wad of blood.

Pushing through the crowd, I passed under the archway. Immediately, I felt the presence of the nexus. All those roads, calling to me. I found the one that I wanted and inhaled, long and deep.

Amkhira came up beside me, their hand latching onto my sleeve again.

I exhaled, breathing the name, and stepped forward.

***

Brysbyland Lane was wide and filled with travelers. The Walkers around us were smears of deep purple and red in an infinite brightness, exhalations and whispers a fierce wind that pulled and pushed at me.

Amkhira was even heavier this time than they had been while traveling Detroit Boulevard. I strained at their weight, my jacket pulled tight. Blindly, I reached out with my free hand, grabbing what might have been an elbow through the cloak.

And they were singing again, thrumming like a hummingbird. The sound raised every hair on my body. At least there was no electricity running across my skin this time; apparently I needed to be in direct contact with Amkhira for that to happen.

I continued to exhale, whispering the name of our destination. Just as my breath ran out, we stepped off the Lane and into the Crossroads of Brysbyland.

Gasping, sucking air, I pressed one hand to my knee. I held tight to Amkhira's elbow.

"Just one minute," I panted.

It was full night here, and a pair of crescent moons hung high in the sky. Smaller than Detroit's nexus, the Crossroads was a wide earthen circle surrounded by undulating hills covered in trees and cottages of grass and adobe and wood. Colorful strings of lights draped each roof, crossing narrow dirt pathways to link one house to the next in a web of red and green and blue. The air smelled of candied fruit and chocolate. Pixin fluttered overhead, giggling in the moonlight, and I could hear Foxin barking and yelping in the hills.

Ah. The Festival of the Moons. That explained the Lane packed with travelers.

"It has been one minute. We should continue."

I rolled my shoulders, inhaling and exhaling several times.

"Walker Brown."

"I heard you."

I tested my grip on Amkhira's elbow, focused on our destination, and carefully exhaled the name *Feitha*.

The Avenue was smaller than its name would indicate, but busy. Walkers crowded around us, some with cargo, others carrying one or two passengers. Amkhira dragged against my arm and shoulder. I leaned forward, straining. Squinting against the brightness and the wind, I focused on

Feitha and my breath and the feel of the road beneath my feet.

Forward. Forward. Step by step by step.

Hummingbird-like humming and thrumming.

Exhale. The name on my breath.

My lungs stuttered.

The road wavered, shifted, split in front of me into a dozen, a hundred, a thousand pathways.

Every civilization has ghost stories. Walkers are no different. We have plenty of horror stories about Walkers lost, cursed to forever wander the roads and never reach their destination; tales of Walkers who lost their breath, lost their focus, and fell, trampled into the roads between worlds by their fellow travelers; fables about Walkers carried away by the wind, tossed and torn by cosmic gales and the breath of Gods and other Walkers.

That wouldn't happen to me.

No.

I reached deep down, deep into my lungs for my last bit of breath. The wind battered my ears, the brightness all around nearly overwhelming me.

Feitha.

We popped into the Crossroads and I collapsed. I couldn't seem to get enough air. I felt like I was starving, my chest tight and hollow.

I don't know how long I sat there before I realized that it was raining. Blue water plunged out of a mauve sky, splattering off my backpack, turning the dirt and grass to sloppy mud. My hair was flat and slicked to my head. My jacket was drenched and I could feel the water slipping beneath my clothes and into my boots.

Monsoon season. No wonder the Avenue had been busy. Walkers were descending on Feitha to collect the fresh rain and carry it over the roads to hundreds of different worlds. I could just make out a host of Hemkirish through the deluge, gigantic open-topped tanks strapped to their backs. There were a few Cervithians, too, delicate painted jugs hanging from their flanks; and Drakes spitting fire, collecting the steam in spiraling glass tubes.

"Walker Brown —"

"Swear to Gods." I glared up at Amkhira, digging my fingers into the mud and trampled grass, blinking against the blue water. It beaded on my eyelashes and ran in thin rivulets down my neck. My clothes stuck to my skin. "I seriously *swear to Gods* — every last one of Them — that if you tell me to get up or that I'm weak or that we must proceed or whatever, I'll ... I'll ...."

I clenched my jaw.

Amkhira had Father's location. They knew where he was.

I had looked for him for years. I couldn't find him on my own.

They had the one thing I truly wanted.

And I, apparently, had the one thing they truly wanted: access to Zerzurrah.

I fell silent.

Amkhira waited.

The rain continued to fall, sometimes straight down, sometimes sideways as the wind kicked up. Walkers popped in and out around us, juggling tanks and jars. A few slipped in the mud as they came and went, swearing in a thousand different languages. Further out, beyond the Crossroads, the grass stretched out in an endless plain, growing taller than Peterrmenn where it hadn't been trampled into the ground.

Finally, when my chest didn't feel quite so tight and hollow, I stood.

I held out my arm. "Hold onto me. I don't think I'll be able to hold onto you."

Amkhira's cracked hand closed around my forearm and squeezed painfully.

"Don't let go," I said, and stepped onto Zerzurrah Avenue.

***

For a few days every year, Zerzurrah Avenue is so filled with travelers that it is almost impossible to move. Greed, pride, envy, hunger, and desire all drive people to the gates of the forbidden city. Untold numbers of Walkers have died trying to reach Zerzurrah, their breath lost, their words carried away on the wind between worlds.

For a moment, I thought the figure in front of me was just such a Walker, long dead, their ghost haunting the roads of creation.

A serpent. Liquid silver, like a skein of silk. Immense, so long that I couldn't see the far end of its tail. Then suddenly comprehensible in size, corkscrewing in the air in front of me. One head, then three, then one again, glimmering.

How very curious.

Words? Spoken? In my head?

It circled around us even as we continued forward, Amkhira's fingers tight around my arm, their weight dragging.

We shall be most curious to see how this develops. How exciting!

And then it was gone, and we stepped onto the Crossroads of Zerzurrah.

I sucked swampy air, coughed, and inhaled again.

I pulled free of Amkhira's grip. "What was that?"

They looked at me, expression blank.

"The big silver snake? You didn't see it?"

Something like fear flitted across their face, and they abruptly floated back, out of reach.

Maybe I had been hallucinating; oxygen deprivation and physical exhaustion. But somehow I doubted it. The serpent had been real and the fact that it had hidden itself from Amkhira was ....

Yet another problem that I didn't have time to worry about.

"We have arrived," they said.

I looked up and around.

It was midmorning, the sky pearly with clouds. The Crossroads of Zerzurrah was a wide circle of hard-packed dirt surrounded on three sides by dense swamp. The trees were green, the shadows between them deepest black. The shadows stretched out, tendrils slithering around the outermost edges of the Crossroads. No one went into the swamp. The idiots who did — trying to find a back way into the city, hunting rare animals or flowers, whatever — never came out.

On the far side of the Crossroads stood the gates and wall of the city. The doors stretched up into the sky, not quite lost to sight, but very nearly. Utterly plain, unadorned wood of a soft golden brown; no handle, no latch, the seam between the two halves only visible if you knew to look for it. The walls were only half as tall, but stretched to either horizon; no one knew how far they went, how big the city really was. Creamy white stone, the walls were covered in ever-shifting, ever-changing reliefs. I recognized the Zerzurrahns themselves and some of the

Deities, but the story was lost to me; it never seemed to be the same twice.

Our arrival had been noted. The edges of the Crossroads were cluttered with huts and stalls, particularly right up against the wall. A few Oscirians, some Neanderthals and Drakes, even a pair of lupine-like Fenrisians. They all stopped what they had been doing to watch us.

"Fulfill your portion of our agreement," Amkhira continued, "and I shall fulfill mine."

"My father, and safe passage home, in exchange for a single page from the *Infinite Atlas*."

Amkhira offered the barest of nods.

"Which page?"

Amkhira darted a glance at our audience, then floated a few inches closer to me.

"You seek the page with my name written upon it."

"Uh." I needed a moment to wrap my head around that. The *Infinite Atlas* was just that: an atlas. It marked places and the routes between places: cities, realms, pocket dimensions, temporal loops and storms of potentiality and cosmic nurseries, roads of every size and description from the broadest boulevards to the narrowest weedy pathway.

Not people.

Amkhira wasn't a people. A person. Amkhira was ... something else. Something that would be named and marked in an atlas.

"Do not linger, Walker Brown."

More pissed off red electricity, tattoos swirling across their face, behind their eyes.

I wondered if Herbert had known, or how much he knew or suspected about Amkhira when he introduced us.

We were going to have a serious talk when I got back to Jerseea.

Jaw tight, I turned and walked out of the Crossroads and up to the gates of Zerzurrah. Eyes watched me the entire way, mostly curious. I heard muttering and guffaws of disbelief as I lifted my hand and knocked against the wood.

The sound was dull and hollow.

Tilting back my head, I called out, "People of Zerzurrah! I, Bertha Brown, Walker, stand at your gate! I, Bertha Brown, Walker, have come in fulfillment of your debt!"

Silence.

More muttering behind me, and it sounded like the Fenrisians were laughing.

I didn't turn around.

Remember when I said that people had tried to buy the pass off both Father and me? Well, we couldn't have sold it even if we had wanted to do so. The pass isn't a physical piece of paper or plastic or metal. It's *me*. *I* am the pass, my soul/mind/heart, my unique psykhé.

Me.

And for me, the gates of Zerzurrah opened.

~ FOUR ~

The gates were nearly silent as they swung inward. I couldn't see the hinges, and I heard only the faintest drag of wood against metal. Slowly. Slowly.

The doors stopped. They hung open just a few feet, barely wide enough for me to slip through without brushing my shoulders on either side.

I could hear and feel the crowd behind me. Every merchant and shopper and loitering tourist had abandoned their huts and wares to push close, muttering and whispering. A few were whimpering or cursing. They shoved against my back, anxious, desperate, trying to see around me, trying to push around me. Hands and paws appeared in my peripheral vision, straining and clawing.

I couldn't see Amkhira.

Another hard shove, my backpack grinding against my wet clothes.

I stumbled forward under the weight of the crowd, passing between the doors. I cast a quick glance over my shoulder. An Oscirian and Fenrisian tried to follow, but they just seemed to ... slide sideways. Every time they tried to take a step forward, they touched something slippery and off they went. A Cervithian tried to jump over them, furred legs flexing, hooves gleaming, and hit the same slippery barrier.

Anxiety and desperation changed to anger. The crowd surged, faces contorting in jealousy. Teeth and fangs flashed as whispers and curses turned to shouts.

The gate closed behind me. Not even a click, just a slight rasp of wood.

Silence.

Pulling my jacket straight, shifting the backpack on my shoulders, I turned my attention to the city that spread out in front of me. And above me. And ... below me.

When I had accidentally found the back road into Zerzurrah, I had popped out in the middle of their hatchery. That had been an enclosed space, dark except for a few high windows, covered in feathers and soft dirt, smelling of honey and dried grass.

This — the city — looked nothing like that.

I wasn't standing on solid ground. I was on a wide walkway that branched to either side, following the walls, and straight ahead, and at an angle up to the right and at another angle down to the left. The walkway was a pale off-white ceramic, like ivory strands loosely woven so that sunlight filtered down and down and down, illuminating even the deepest depths of the city.

It felt odd beneath my wet boots, tinging with each step as I moved forward, staring around me in awe. My mouth was probably hanging open.

Towers rose in and among the walkways, twisting and spiraling. Ceramic, or maybe bone or eggshell, varying from rusty orange to dark yellow to russet brown; the colors shifted, flowing in and out of one another. Delicate, fragile, riddled with holes that might have been doors or windows.

I heard wings. A shadow passed overhead.

I looked up, squinting against the drops of sunlight.

A Zerzurrahn landed in front of me, hind legs first, then middle legs, then front legs. Both pairs of wings fluttered once and then folded neatly along its back. The feathered comb atop its head was upright with agitation and curiosity. A mixture of scales, fur, and feathers, all deep blue edging towards purple, covered its body. Golden claws, a golden beak, golden eyes, and a tail nearly as long as its body that ended in a tuft of golden feathers.

"Walker Bertha Brown, I speak on behalf of the Nest. On behalf of the Nest, and all who are blessed to hatch within its walls, I welcome you. Walker Brown, you may address me as Chharhan."

I bowed low, eyes dropping to the walkway. My backpack shifted uncomfortably, dragging at my wet clothes, and I rolled my shoulders in a futile attempt to move it back into place. "Chharhan, I am honored by the welcome offered by you on behalf of the Nest, and all who are blessed to hatch within its walls."

The Zerzurrahn dipped its head and bent its two front legs, returning my greeting. The words that followed were a statement, a binding proclamation, not a question. "Walker Brown, you have come in fulfillment of our debt to you."

"I have. This day shall see the fulfillment of the Nest's debt to me."

Chharhan blinked slowly, eyes shading from deep gold to something closer to canary and back again. It settled on its four back legs, wings still folded close, feathered comb relaxing against its head.

No movement around us. No other Zerzurrahns anywhere within my sight.

Chharhan was seated in a calm, conversational pose. I had seen this plenty of times on market day, when Zerzurrahns wandered out into the crossroads to negotiate with merchants or exchange morsels of information with scholars.

But Chharhan wasn't really calm and relaxed. No. The Zerzurrahns wanted me in and out as quickly as possible, and would reveal as little to me about themselves and their city as they could.

I drew a deep breath, slowly exhaling. "I wish to purchase four items, and I bring fair recompense in exchange."

Chharhan dipped its head again, motioning for me to continue.

I pulled the bag of Herbert's coins from inside my shirt, tugging it open to spill the gold into one palm. "In exchange for three whole Zerzurrahn egg shells."

Chharhan studied the coins for a moment, then nodded. "It is agreed."

I dumped the coins back into the pouch and set it down on the ground, roughly halfway between us. I reached into my shirt again and pulled out the fine, light cloth with the amber tear tucked inside.

Chharhan's feather comb twitched.

I gently unfolded the cloth and held it out so that the tear was clearly visible. It shone a soft golden-brown in the sunlight, the dark specks within casting minute shadows over the white cloth.

"In exchange for one page from the *Infinite Atlas*."

The feather comb shot straight up, and then Chharhan went very still.

It stared at me.

I stared back.

Chharhan rose slowly onto all six feet, golden claws making a harsh grating sound against the ivory walkway. It paced towards me, glaring down over its beak.

"And this will fulfill our debt to you, Walker Brown."

Another binding statement.

"Three whole egg shells and one page of my choice from the *Infinite Atlas* — yes. The Nest's debt will be fulfilled."

Another silence with more staring.

Sweat trickled down my back and my arm started to cramp, but I didn't look away.

My father. I almost had my father back. I couldn't lose now.

"It is agreed." One more step forward, so that Chharhan was looming over me, sharp golden beak a hair's breadth from my forehead. "But hear this well, Walker Brown, as I speak on behalf of the Nest, and all who are blessed to hatch within its walls: never again will you be welcome at our gates, or at our crossroads, nor will any whom you guide to our realm. Do you understand my words?"

I tilted my chin so that Chharhan's beak now pointed down at my nose, and we were eye to eye.

"Yes, I understand your words. I heed and comprehend, and I accede."

Chharhan's rear wings flashed and fluttered, and it pranced backwards a few steps. "Leave the coins and the tear. You will follow me, and you will not deviate from the path I walk."

I crouched, laying the tear and its cloth next to the pouch. When I straightened, Chharhan was already a good twenty feet away, its six legs setting a quick pace. I scrambled, jogging to catch up, the ivory walkway tinging musically beneath my boots.

***

As a Walker, I knew how to navigate the roads of creation. I instinctively felt the pathways and how they interconnected. That talent extended to cities and towns, to a certain extent. I didn't have the same instinctive understanding of mundane roadways, but I figured out the pattern pretty quickly; faster than non-Walkers.

Even when I was lost, I was never really *lost*.

In Zerzurrah, I was utterly and completely *lost*.

Chharhan led me up one walkway and down another, through swooping loops and around winding bends. Other than the city wall — which was quickly gone from my sight — there wasn't a single right angle anywhere. It was all curves and swirls.

And it was completely quiet. And ... scentless, unlike the hatchery. My nose still hurt, but the blood had cleared.

There was nothing here that might be considered greenery. No trees or shrubs or flowers. No birds chirping, no insects buzzing. No traffic of any sort, not on wheels or tracks, or flying overhead.

At one point, I caught a hint of movement in one of the ... windows? Doors? No glass, just open space. That made sense for a species that could fly. The figure I spotted, only for a moment, was clearly Zerzurrahn, but much smaller. And it lacked wings.

Maybe that was the reason for the walkways. Their young couldn't fly.

"I will not mention the *Atlas*."

Chharhan slowed, one golden eye peering back at me.

"The location of the *Infinite Atlas* is meant to be secret. It is not a secret I will share."

The Zerzurrahn blinked slowly, then nodded and turned away.

And we kept walking.

***

The tower that Chharhan led me into looked no different than any other: a fat spiral of rust and dark yellow and russet that went down and down and up and up. We entered somewhere near the middle, the room before us spreading out to the far walls. The floor was the same mixture of colors as the exterior, and translucent enough to allow sunlight to pass through from one level to the next.

Looking up, I saw faint shadows. Figures, other Zerzurrahns, moving around on the level above us, but silently and out of direct sight.

"The *Infinite Atlas*," Chharhan announced.

Dragging my attention away from the ceiling, I refocused on the space around us. The very empty space, except for a single bookstand. It grew directly out of the floor, delicate tendrils curling, in the very center of the room. It was tall, too. The *Atlas* sat above my head, high enough for an adult Zerzurrahn to read.

Chharhan sat on its rear legs, all its claws still extended. Its feather comb bobbed up and down.

"Thank you."

No response.

Licking my lips, I walked over to the bookstand. My boots squeaked. Grimacing at the ugly sound, I looked up at the *Atlas* for a moment. I could just see the edge of the bottom cover. I could reach it, but I somehow doubted that

Chharhan and the rest of the Zerzurrahns would approve of me pulling the *Atlas* down and spreading it out on the ground.

Shrugging my shoulders, I tugged off my backpack and set it on the floor. It didn't contain anything fragile or valuable now. I had delivered every bottle of Hy-Brasil whiskey and Kitezh caviar to Herbert, plus the bottle of Oscirian berry wine to Peterrmenn. All that was in there now were a few changes of clothes and basic survival supplies like a fire kit and a compact rebreather.

It might be enough to support my weight if I stood on the corners ....

Grabbing the lip of the bookstand for stability, I carefully hoisted myself atop my backpack. The corners crushed slightly, but pushed me up high enough that I could see over the edge, see the *Infinite Atlas* itself.

It was a book. A plain brown book, no markings on the cover or spine, maybe an inch thick, but tall; like a book of fold-out maps.

And it contained infinity.

And I had to find the one page that showed Amkhira's name.

Maybe that would finally tell me what, exactly, Amkhira was.

Assuming I could find it. In all that infinity.

I bit the inside of my lip.

Atlas. A book of maps. A book of places, of heres and theres and whens and wheres, and the ways to get to all of them.

And I was a Walker. I understood the ways to get to here and there and when and where.

Amkhira. I needed to find Amkhira.

I inhaled, long and slow, letting my gaze go unfocused,

the cover of the *Atlas* turning a hazy brown. Exhalation. Another long inhalation and exhalation. Then another. This time, when I exhaled, I bent slightly so that my breath ghosted across the cover.

And I whispered the name.

Amkhira.

I continued to exhale, keeping my focus on the *Atlas*, on the name, on the place.

The cover fluttered. Fluttered again, lifted, and fell open. Pages turned, one after another, flipping by so quickly that they were a blur of blue and black and white and gold. Page after page after page, yet I never seemed to get any closer to the end.

Infinity within the covers of a book.

My lungs got tight as I continued to exhale, whispering the name.

The pages turned.

Exhale. Breathe the name.

My chest started to hurt. I clutched at the edge of the bookstand.

Exhale, name, flip-flip flipflipflip.

Spots danced around the corners of my vision.

The *Atlas* went still.

I gasped, dragging air into my lungs. Blinking rapidly, I flexed my cramped fingers and tried not to fall as the corners of my backpack sagged further under my weight.

Amkhira.

Amkhira wasn't a person.

A map covered the right-hand page. Solid blue with black and white and gold and silver lines that shimmered as they carved through the cosmos, with dots of various sizes where the lines intersected; the more lines that intersected, the bigger the dot. Tiny, perfect script identified each line and dot. I didn't know that language, I had never seen it before, but I could still understand it.

Brulein Avenue and Brulein. The Veitie Crossroads. Yanover Boulevard and Yanover City. Fiorenzia and its tiny pathway that would be clogged with tourists come rainbow season.

And there, in the upper right corner. A dashed white line. The name had been crossed through, but was still legible.

Amkhira Street.

The dashed line led to an end point.

Amkhira.

A tiny dot. Not a crossroads, but a place with only a single road. A pocket universe, maybe, or a time-space fold. One rarely visited. Or not visited at all.

A forbidden road. To a forbidden place.

I swallowed, or tried to do so. My throat was dry.

I lifted a shaking hand, smoothing it over the left page. More perfect neat script in a language that I had never seen but could still read. Each road and crossroads and endpoint was named, followed by a short description. Brulein, a world of perpetual winter where herds of furry brul fought for dominance by singing the ice into exquisite sculptures. The Veitie Crossroads, sitting at the heart of a breathable nebula and if you weren't careful you would float right out of it into open space. Yanover City, a single skyscraper on a single island in the middle of an endless black sea.

The dashed line stretched out from the Veitie Crossroads to that nothing endpoint.

I traced a finger down the list.

Amkhira Street and Amkhira. Both were crossed out, followed by a single word description.

Transitional.

What did that mean?

A tiny silver serpent slid across the page, under my fingers, and across the map, so quickly that it was a streak of light.

I lurched in surprise, almost losing my balance. A corner of my backpack crunched. Grabbing at the bookstand, I pulled myself back upright.

The silver snake whirled around the map and off the edge of the page.

I thought I heard laughter.

"You have found that which you desire, Walker Brown, yes?"

I cleared my throat. "Uh, yes, Chharhan, I have."

"Then remove the map and let us conclude our business."

Remove the map? Literally?

I studied the inner binding. No perforations.

No sign of the snake, either.

Well. Okay.

I grasped the upper right corner with my fingers and very gently began to pull. There were no objections from Chharhan, so I kept pulling.

No tearing sound. Only a low popping, like stitches being pulled free.

In a few seconds, I held the map loose in my hands. I gaped at it, astonishment making my palms sweat.

A flutter and a flip.

I looked up just in time to see a new page slip right back into its place. A duplicate. Exactly the same.

The cover lifted and the pages rolled over. With a soft thunk, the *Infinite Atlas* closed.

***

There was another Zerzurrahn waiting for us at the gate; deep green fur and feathers and scales, with a bronze beak, eyes and tail tuft. This one didn't introduce itself, or speak to me at all. It just held out a tall cylinder with one clawed paw.

Three whole egg shells, carefully stacked atop one another and held in place inside a lattice of ivory-like strands.

I lifted the cylinder, allowing sunlight to pass through the shells. They were completely hollow; they were either dud eggs or their contents had been removed through some means that left the shells intact.

Holding the cylinder in the crook of my elbow, I bowed my thanks to the green and bronze Zerzurrahn.

No acknowledgement at all.

"This concludes our business, Walker Bertha Brown." Chharhan's tail and feather comb twitched.

"It does." I could feel the *Atlas* page where I had rolled it up and tucked it inside my shirt. At least my clothes had finally dried. "The Nest's debt to me is fulfilled. I shall not speak of what I saw here today, nor shall I set foot upon the Crossroads of Zerzurrah again."

"Indeed not, Walker Brown."

The gates swung open, the massive, sky-high golden-brown doors hardly making a sound; again, there was only the faintest rasp of wood against metal.

I moved back a few steps, giving the doors room. They stopped when the gap was just a bit wider than my shoulders.

Business suits. There was a herd of angry business suits.

Baldy glared at me. Bite marks covered his face, one of his ears was half torn away, and there were slashes and rips in his clothing. The dozen other suits arrayed to either side of him, an arc that covered the entire gateway, looked just as bad.

And just as angry.

"Uh," I said.

"Our business, Walker Brown, is concluded." Chharhan paced closer, both sets of wings fluttering, eyes heating to molten gold. It stretched its neck closer, beak clacking.

And then it hissed at me.

The green and bronze Zerzurrahn hissed, too.

I spun as the air was suddenly filled with hissing and clicking and clacking and chirruping. The sounds came from everywhere, above and below and behind me, over-lapping, dissonant. Every hair on my body stood on end, and I instinctively hunched my shoulders and crouched.

Chharhan was on top of me, beak slicing towards me, wings flapping hard. I backpedaled, feet tripping as I scrambled to keep out of its reach. Its wings beat at my head and shoulders, and its beak just narrowly missed my cheek and ear.

And then I was through the gate.

I spun, pressing my crunched backpack to the wood as the doors closed soundlessly.

The crossroads was very quiet. The merchants and shoppers and lingering tourists and scholars huddled around the edges of the open space, sheltering in their huts and tents. They watched, some looking eager, others afraid.

They would offer no assistance.

Where was Amkhira?

Baldy tilted his chin. "Missed you in Detroit. We are here to personally escort you back to Jerseea. Our employer would like to make you an ... alternative offer for the eggs."

"I get the distinct impression that a *yes* or *no* on my part doesn't really matter."

Baldy grinned. A tuft of white fur was caught between two of his front teeth. "You would be correct."

A flutter of red, far off to my right, in the pooling shadows of the jungle.

"Well in that case —"

Amkhira appeared at my side, red electricity crackling across their scalp and hair, down their cheeks and throat. They wrapped that semblance of a half-melted hand around my arm, squeezing hard. I saw Baldy's eyes go wide, his hand start to reach for something inside his jacket.

Every color I had ever seen and a thousand, a million more that I couldn't name. Silence, profound and utterly terrifying. Up and down and sideways and every direction in between, except that I wasn't moving.

We stopped.

I was screaming again, on my knees, the container of eggs clutched against my side.

Amkhira tightened their grip, digging into my skin.

Shouting. The sounds of running.

I pried my eyes open.

We were on the far side of the crossroad, opposite the gate. As far as we could possibly get from Zerzurrah without moving into the swamp or leaving the realm entirely.

Baldy and his fellow suits were running towards us. Guns. Knives. Hooks. They were angry and yelling.

"Don'let go," I whispered.

I pushed to my feet, inhaled, and exhaled the name. *Veitie.* And I stepped onto the road.

~ FIVE ~

THE VEITIE CROSSROADS WERE ANCIENT; SO OLD THAT THERE were no historical records of its discovery, only legends. In one story, Hermes and Mercurius had guided a lost Walker to safety there just as she was about to run out of breath. In another, a family of Walkers had kept the Crossroads a secret for generations until one had a falling out with his kin; when they realized that he had shared the secret, they dragged him home and shoved his body out of the nebula and into the cold of space; it was still floating out there.

My favorite story was the one Father had shared with me, a bedtime tale whispered when all four of us — Father and Mother and Grandmother and I — would pitch a tent on the roof of our apartment building and camp out under the stars. He would point to one and say, "Maybe that star will be a Crossroad someday."

Because that's how Veitie came to be. A sun near the end of its life. The few planets that spun around it had never birthed any life, not even bacteria. But the sun wanted more, felt that it could be more, do more. So the star prayed and the Gods heard its plea. When the sun exploded in its death throes, it was transformed. The energy and heat and light of its death bent space, pulling and tugging and twisting the nearest roads until they curved and came together.

The Veitie Crossroads, the final breath and prayer of a dead star. A weightless cloud of green and purple. Scattered bits of rock covered in bioluminescent moss and flowers float through the cloud, golden chains strung between them to create pathways and nets. Safe havens for the merchants and traders and explorers and scholars who gather there to exchange goods and stories.

I only knew that we had arrived because I could breathe again. My vision was spotty and dark, my ears buzzed with a loud hummingbird hum, and I felt chilled. My whole body was shaking, and my shoulder and arm ached.

I flailed. Something grabbed my sore arm, guided my hand.

I felt a chain under my fingers and I latched on tight.

My clothes floated up around me and I could feel the weight change as my hair lifted free of my shoulders and scalp. I almost lost my hold on the eggs in their ceramic lattice.

I clung to that chain and gradually, too slowly, my vision cleared and the buzzing in my ears faded. Blinking, I looked around.

The nebula's striking colors were only visible from a distance. Immediately around me, it was clear, and I had a good view of the Crossroads.

Not surprisingly, our appearance had attracted no interest whatsoever. Everyone was far too busy going about their own business. Neanderthals and Cervithians and other sentients followed hundreds of chains, from one netted area to the next, their safety lines locked into place.

Pixin scampered along the golden links, carrying messages and small packages. One jumped over my hand, running, translucent wings fluttering. It looked like they had converted several of the floating rocks into habitats, because I could see Pixin cocoons dangling from the bioluminescent flowers. A massive Drake, the largest I had ever seen, clung to the outside of a net, arguing through the chains with a pair of Foxin. The Drake's breath steamed, and the Foxins' ears and tails had fluffed in agitation. A Neanderthal growled at me in annoyance as he passed, unclipping and re-clipping his safety line to get around me.

Oops. Safety line.

Damn. No rope and clamp in my backpack.

Well, I would just have to be very very careful and not lose my grip.

Amkhira floated into my line of sight. They had pulled their cloak tight and curled up what might have been their legs. The end result was that they looked like a bouncing red ball with a black bump for a head.

I almost laughed. Amkhira's grim expression stopped me.

"You have the map from the *Infinite Atlas*?"

My momentary good humor disappeared. "I do."

That burnt hand shot out from between the folds of their cloak. "Give it to me."

I hesitated.

"If you would see your father again, *give it to me*."

I hesitated again, and red electricity crackled down the sides of Amkhira's face and neck. A Pixin running along the chain towards us squeaked in alarm, turned around, and raced back towards their habitat.

I tucked the container of eggs under my arm. With my free hand, I felt inside my shirt and pulled out the roll of the map. I held it between my fingers, but did not extend it to Amkhira.

"Are you a Forbidden Road?"

They glared at me. This time, the electricity spat and skated along the surface of their cloak. For a moment, they looked like a sphere of angry red lightning. I had to squint my eyes against the intensity of the glow.

The chain vibrated beneath my hands. I twisted my head to see a Hemkirish and a few Cervithians turning, dragging themselves away, making for the nearest net. Pixin watched, wide-eyed, from a boulder, the bioluminescent flowers shivering.

A bolt of electricity hit the chain, turning it red and hot. I hissed at the flash of pain, let go, started to float —

— I corkscrewed, made a mad grab, caught the chain again.

"I have been denied myself, my nature sundered. Ripped. Shattered. No more! *Give me the map!*"

More angry red lightning. It crashed through the nebula, striking the net where the Drake and Foxin had ceased their arguing to stare in shock and surprise. When the electricity hit, the Foxins' fur stood on end and the Drake convulsed, releasing its hold. I could hear the Pixin screaming right at the edge of my hearing, the sound so high that my teeth hurt and my eyes watered.

The Drake flailed, tail snapping, and just managed to catch the net before it floated out of reach.

"Stop!"

More lightning, and a boulder shattered, scattering debris and moss and flowers. A Pixin cocoon whipped past my head.

"Amkhira, stop!" I thrust the map towards them, my face turned away. "Here! Take it!"

That hummingbird thrum beat against me and the crackle of electricity was loud as Amkhira moved closer. They didn't float uncontrollably or flail madly. They simply glided towards me. When they were close enough, they snatched the map away, their burned and blackened and melted hand slamming against my fingers.

I gasped, the sting vibrating up my wrist and forearm, and curled my hand protectively against my chest.

The map unrolled. The page glowed, turning transparent. For an instant, I could see the map and Amkhira and the nebula and the stars beyond, all layered on top of one another.

"Speak my name."

I drew a breath.

"Amkhira."

The map caught flame, turned to light, and disappeared.

Amkhira's cloak flared wide, spreading and growing, extending outward until that was all I could see. The nebula was gone. There was only a great wall of red and lightning and flame. And, within that red, a bundle of black. A mass of tar curled in on itself, lumpy, almost pitiful.

And then that, too, began to grow.

The tar bubbled, oozing out, lengthening. Red and gold highlights appeared, slipping down through the tar like neon paint.

The road that was Amkhira flattened, widened, sinking into the mass/matter/energy of creation. The red and gold highlights spun, whirling into spheres, then flattening into circles. The road that was Amkhira sank further, merging with the universe. The circles continued to spin, circles within circles, filled with that language that I recognized and could understand deep down in my soul.

"Walk."

Amkhira's voice, but no longer rough and gravelly. Smooth, hot.

Breathe. Exhale.

I took a step forward. The road that was Amkhira was solid beneath my feet, and the circles continued to spin slowly. There was no infinite brightness here, no wind that was the breath of Gods and Walkers. I could hear the beating of my own heart, feel the deflation of my lungs as I continued to exhale. The air was warm and heavy, and reddish embers glowed all around me.

Breathe. Exhale. Speak the name.

How long was this road? Would I have enough breath to reach the end?

And what would I find if I did?

I looked down, the words within the circles catching my eye. A story. No, not just a story. A history. A biography. The story of Amkhira.

The first road.

I stopped, wobbling on my feet.

The first road —

Yes, quite curious and exciting, indeed.

The serpent again, a brilliant streak of silver against the blackness and the embers and the golden circles. It twirled in the air, incomprehensibly large. One head, then three, then one again.

Out of all the probable outcomes, this is my fourth favorite.

The embers and circles blurred, my lungs straining. The name faded from my lips and became nothing.

The silver serpent shrank, corkscrewing around me. I could breathe again. I panted, sucking in air, utterly unable to understand why I was still here. How I was still here, and not ... lost. My focus had been broken, the name interrupted. I should be tumbling through creation, unable to stop myself or save myself.

Yes, but I won't allow that. At least not this time.

The serpent shifted form and color. He was a melanistic fox now, as big as a horse, the cinnamon-red and black of his fur perfectly matching the road and the embers that floated through the air. Golden-orange eyes studied me.

You do possess a most unusual ability to find that which has been lost or hidden. Or forbidden.

"I — I —"

A God. I was speaking to a God. What else could he be?

Correct. The fox leaned towards me. *Mortals do not see very well. Most mortals, anyway. Perhaps that is your secret. Before, you were almost completely blind. Now, you are only mostly blind. Your comprehension of creation is fractionally better.*

"Thank you?"

The fox twitched an ear. *Why would you thank me? I haven't done anything. No, this is all on you. I should warn you, however, that mortals whose eyes are opened rarely do well after the fact. They have difficulty reconciling what they knew to be true with what they know to be true, what they once saw with what they now see. I do hope that you avoid insanity.*

My mouth opened and closed soundlessly.

The fox shifted, shrinking into the form of a normal-sized raccoon.

He folded his hands across his pot belly. *I offer you this word of warning, as well. Amkhira **is** a Forbidden Road. Always and forever. Despite that, curious mortals kept finding their way here. We couldn't have that, now could we? Something had to be done.*

"Wh-what? Why?"

Well, because Amkhira leads back to the beginning.

I cleared my throat. "The beginning of what?"

The raccoon scowled at me in disappointment. *Why,* **everything**, *of course.*

He changed again, becoming a massive black tortoise. Golden circles similar to those on the road spun on the panels of his shell, while another rotated in the air above his head. As I watched, red lightning cracked, jumping from one rim of the circle to the other.

The embers all around me shivered. A few dropped to the road that was Amkhira, melting into the asphalt. There was a bubbling and hissing. And then, with a growly, satisfied hum, they exploded outward, stretching, forming narrow roads. A few intersected one another here and there, while others extended off into infinity.

The tortoise turned his massive head towards one of the newborn roads. He smiled.

Yes. That one. I shall explore that road.

The tortoise shrank. He became a mouse, fur a silvery white, barely the size of my palm.

He leapt, scampering until he reached that new road. He turned back towards me, ears and nose twitching.

I shall call this road ... Berthain. An homage, but not so similar that the universe gets confused. That is never a good thing. The God who was a mouse tilted his head at me. *As I said, this is my fourth favorite probable outcome. Depending on the decision you make next, this could become my second favorite. Or my least favorite.*

"How — how will —" I swallowed and found my voice. "How will I know?"

The God lifted onto his rear legs.

You won't.

And then he scampered away, disappearing into infinity.

***

I walked. I walked and I walked, and I kept walking. I had no sense of the passage of time. I wasn't hungry or thirsty. Or tired. But I was sore. My shoulder and arm still ached from dragging Amkhira's weight from one crossroad to another, and my hand tingled from touching the electrified chain in Veitie.

At one point, I slipped off my backpack and carefully tucked the container of eggs inside.

I continued to follow Amkhira Street, avoiding the criss-crossing and branching avenues that angled in from every direction and then away. Away and away, into forever.

I felt ... weird when I crossed those intersections. They were crossroads. They had to be.

Mortals do not see very well. That is what the God had said — whichever God he was.

I looked around me, at the dark road and the golden circles with their histories and the embryonic roads hovering like embers.

Is this what it all really looked like? Or was this only *closer* to what it really looked like? Were the infinite brightness and the wind and the strange forms of the other Walkers just ... an illusion? No, that wasn't right. Not an illusion. More like, an approximation. This, all of this that I was seeing now as I traversed the first road, was a slightly more accurate approximation. A mortal's limited comprehension of the infinity of creation.

Amkhira Street led everywhere, touched everything. Every here and there, every where and when.

I read bits and pieces of Amkhira's history as I walked. I didn't understand most of it. Not because I had suddenly lost the ability to comprehend this strange language, but because I didn't recognize any of the names; aside from that of Amkhira, anyway. Their name was everywhere. But the rest? Were they people? Places? Events? Gods? So-and-so came here, so-and-so went there. This name walked here, that name traveled there. These names walked together and then parted company. This name came into being, that name ceased to be. This name is now connected to that name.

Wait.

I knew that name: Kryzkaltislk. And Mercurius. Then more that I didn't understand.

And then a name that I did recognize.

Jeremiah Allendale Brown of Detroit.

And the road came to an end.

~ SIX ~

At first, I couldn't understand what I was seeing. What I was hearing and smelling.

I was home. I was back in our apartment in Detroit.

Grandmother was in her favorite chair, book in hand, comfy bunny slippers on, feet propped up on the coffee table. Mother was over by the big window, dusting and misting her plants.

That ... wasn't right. The coffee table had been replaced several years ago. The plants were long gone. Mother hadn't been able to care for them after increasing her hours driving her cab, and had given them to Aselolla. The couch was wrong, too.

This was all old. The way the apartment had looked when I was a child.

Before Father had disappeared.

He came through the door of the kitchen, balancing several plates of pancakes and bacon on his arms. His fingers were curled awkwardly through the handles of a jar of Oscirian syrup and a jug of Pohjolan milk.

"Breakfast is up! Get it while it's hot!"

My breath caught on a sob.

He looked exactly the same. Almost twenty years, and he hadn't aged at all. Not so much as a day. Same curly black hair, same dark skin, same wide smile. Same scar on the left side of his forehead, where he had tripped chasing me around the living room and fallen against the coffee table.

"Father?" My voice was barely above a whisper. "Father?"

No reaction as he set the plates down on the dining room table.

I watched as Mother smiled and tucked away her mister and duster to take her seat. Grandmother just hummed, laid her bookmark in place, and set her book down on her chair.

Down the hallway, I heard a door bang open, and eight year-old me skipped into the room.

Me. The exact age I was when Father disappeared.

"Pancakes!" other me squealed in delight, and scrambled into a dining room chair. I stabbed a fork into a circle of hot, fluffy dough and dragged it onto my plate.

Father cleared his throat, settling in beside me.

Other me dropped her fork with a clatter, tucking her chin against her chest.

Father smiled with affection, winked at Mother, and turned to Grandmother. "Mom, care to do the honors?"

Grandmother nodded. "I would love to."

She held out her hands and we formed a circle, fingers intertwined. "Gracious Hermes, loving Ganesh, and all you Gods who watch over the roads and those who travel upon them. We thank you for those who produced this fare, and for those who walked the roads to bring it to us. We thank you for protecting Jeremiah in his travels, and for bringing him home to us safely, as you have guided home so many others."

A moment of silence, and then other me and this other family dug into the pancakes, chewing happily.

I took a hesitant step forward and tried again. "Father?"

Still no reaction. No one looked up or so much as twitched in my direction.

I moved around the table, edging past my eight year-old self. At that age, I had just started to grow out my hair, the long strands held back by a series of pink barrettes. I would keep growing it for several more years, convinced that if I cut it, Father would never come home. A childish superstition that I finally abandoned when I went off for my first formal apprenticeship.

"Father?"

I stopped beside his chair and waved my hand in front of his face.

He blinked, seemed to hesitate as he lifted the fork full of pancake.

My breath caught and I leaned closer, snapping my fingers.

He frowned.

"Father!" Flexing my hand, I tentatively reached out and touched his shoulder.

He flinched and looked around, then squirmed and rolled his shoulder.

The other three people at the table — Grandmother, Mother, little me — stilled, forks paused.

I squeezed. "Jeremiah!" I yelled, leaning towards him. "Jeremiah Allendale Brown!"

He flinched again and the room around us wavered, like a snow globe that had been jiggled.

This time I grabbed both of his shoulders, shaking him

so hard that he dropped his fork. Syrup splashed on his shirt. The bag rattled against my back. I was yelling, screaming "Father! Jeremiah!" over and over again.

He gasped. His eyes widened and he blinked, gaze slowly coming to focus on me. A terrible sound, horrified, anguished, ripped up his throat. He fell back, his chair tipping. He landed hard on his back and scrambled awkwardly to his feet, hands held out in front of him as if to ward me off.

"Father? Father, no, don't —"

His eyes were wide and panicked now and he was shaking his head. He pressed his hands over his ears, muttering, "No, no, no. You can't. Good thoughts. Keep good —"

The room around us disappeared, splashing away like watercolor paint. The walls, ceiling, window, furniture. The other me and the other Grandmother and other Mother. All gone. For a moment, we were inside a rainbow, light and color coming from every direction.

Then it all changed again. We were ... I looked around ... twin full moons high in the sky. Rolling hills of tropical forest and cute little cottages of wood and grass.

Brysbyland. And everything was on fire. The cottages, the trees, the grass. Thick smoke obscured the moons. The heat from the fire rapidly warmed my skin. I would start to blister soon, and the smoke was already clogging my nose and lungs.

Father was moaning, hands still wrapped around his ears. "Bad thoughts, bad thoughts."

A dark shape loomed up in front of me and I lurched away in surprise.

Baldy. But a monstrous version of him: his eyes too big, his smile sharp, his long arms reaching for Father.

"No!" I lunged around Baldy, putting myself between him and Father. The flames roared higher, loud and hissing and crackling, and the smoke thickened. I started coughing. "Father! Focus! Focus on me, Father!"

He shook his head, backing away. "Good. Think good. Happy. Happy happy happy ...."

I followed after him. "Home! Think of home."

Baldy grabbed me from behind and squeezed hard, cutting off my scream.

And then he was gone, and so was burning Brysbyland. It sloughed away. For a moment, we were floating inside a rainbow again. And then the apartment reappeared around us. Mostly. It was off-kilter, the angles weird; like a child's drawing. And still filled with old furniture and plants.

Father was on his knees, rocking back and forth, his eyes squeezed shut. "Good good good happy happy happy ...."

I carefully dropped down in front of him, and gently laid a hand on his shoulder. I remained quiet and still, waiting.

Eventually, his rocking slowed and his eyes cracked open. He blinked when he saw me. He drew a ragged breath. "You're real. You're really here."

"Yes. Yes, I am." I spoke slowly, clearly, softly. "We used to camp on the roof and you would tell me stories about the stars. You hate Mother's pancakes, but you never told her, just said that you liked to make them yourself. Grandmother loves Cervithian fudge, and you would go there every year and buy a box for her birthday, and she would share, and we'd spend the whole day eating it and then complain about our stomach aches .... I'm *me*. Bertha Mazarine Brown. Your daughter."

He flinched, but didn't pull away.

And then he grabbed me, yanking me into a bone-crushing hug. I could feel the strength of his hug through the ridged backpack. His tears were running into my hair, and I was crying, too, as he chanted, "My beautiful girl. My beautiful baby girl."

Found him. I found him.

"My beautiful girl. I'm so sorry. I'm so sorry that I missed you growing up. I'm so sorry."

After all these years, I had found my father. I was crying so hard that my chest and throat hurt.

"How long? How long have I been gone?"

We could go home, be a family again, I could just see the expression on Mother and Grandmother's faces, hear the joy in their voices —

Blinking through my tears, I realized that the living room had changed again. The angles were correct now, not off kilter. The plants were gone, and the coffee table and the couch were the new ones we had just purchased a few years ago. This was the home that I knew, the home of my adulthood.

And Mother and Grandmother looked exactly as I had left them, Mother with her braids and Grandmother with her fuzzy slippers. They were smiling and weeping, and Grandmother was just shaking her head. Mother kept whispering between her sobs, "You found him, oh Bertha, you found him. Just like you promised."

"Yes, I did." I smiled back at them. My cheeks still felt wet. I lifted my head from Father's chest. "I told you that I would find him —"

"Bertha, stop."

Father's voice was firm, edging towards panic.

I frowned at him. "What? Father, we're home! I brought you home!"

"No, baby girl." He shook his head, fingers squeezing tight around my arms. "Not yet. We need to leave. *Now.*"

What was he talking about? I gestured towards Grandmother and Mother. The front door opened, and Aselolla came in, her skin the deep blue of delight, her four hands clutching flowers and balloons. Branson followed, smiling, hat tucked under his arm, the brass buttons on his long jacket winking in the sunlight. "But —"

"No, daughter. Do you hear me?"

"I don't understand. No. We're finally home — no — we're not leaving!" I jerked, pulling myself free.

Grandmother and Mother were talking, crying, joy turned to confusion and pain, asking Father why he wanted to abandon us again. Why? Why did he want to leave them?

The light coming through the windows faded, and I heard thunder. I could hear running footsteps in the hallway, too, a horde in black business suits carrying guns and knives and hooks. Aselolla had changed colors again, this time a sickening orange, and Branson was dead on the floor, beaten and bloody. Grandmother and Mother were yelling now, furious with me, screaming that I was a disappointment. Fear and shame made my heart pound.

"I'm not going to let you make the same terrible mistake that I did." Father grabbed my arm, latching on tight. He spun me around, locking eyes. "We need to leave, while we still can. You found this place, deliberately, not accidentally. You found it, you can *unfind* it. You are a *Walker*, Bertha Mazarine Brown. It's in your blood, your brain, your soul. Say the name, and *walk*." He drew a breath, his other arm around my waist.

I focused, blocking out the fear and the shame and the shouting. I inhaled, breathed the name —*"Amkhira"* — and stepped forward.

***

We walked. We walked for a long time, though for how long I couldn't say. Amkhira Street was solid beneath our feet. We kept our course, avoiding the other roads that criss-crossed and branched in every direction. That strange script, the history/biography of Amkhira — of everyone and everything that the street touched, the story of creation — swirled and circled, and the reddish embers that were embryonic roads floated in the darkness all around us.

We talked. We talked for a long time. Father wept when I told him how long he had been gone, how much he had missed, how we had never stopped loving him.

We fell silent, my arm curled through the crook of his elbow.

The road stretched ahead of us and behind us, forever.

"How did you end up there? How did you get to ... um, the beginning?" I asked.

"The beginning?" He hesitated. "Yes, I suppose that's as good a name for it as any."

"That's what the God called it. The beginning of everything."

Father peered down at me. "Met a God, did you? Which one?"

I just shrugged.

"Well, to answer your question, I was running. Some individuals whom I had no interest in interacting with were following me. They were ... persistent. I eluded them several times, but they kept finding me again. So, I thought I would be clever. Tricky. I did what you did, though consciously instead of by instinct."

I tilted my head to look up at him. "You found an unknown road."

"Ehn," he grunted, an unhappy sound. "Walker instincts fueled by desperation and arrogance. I didn't find just an unknown road. I found a *Forbidden Road*." He hesitated again, then lifted a hand, gesturing at the swirling script and the embers hanging in the air. "It didn't look like this. It looked like every other road. But it was quiet. Empty. Only me. I walked until I ran out of breath, and I found myself at the end — the beginning — whatever you want to call it." He squeezed my arm. "It changed. It kept changing. Responded to every random thought that went through my head, conscious or unconscious. Good — and bad. Whatever I imagined became real. Raw potential shaped by my mind."

"You imagined home."

His smile was more of a painful grimace. "I couldn't figure out how to leave, how to save myself. Eventually, I figured out how to keep my focus, how to hold that one good thought in my head. After lots of ... very bad things. And then, I don't know how much later, for a single terrible, lucid moment, Amkhira appeared. They were there ... fractions of a second, maybe less. They were being torn apart, they said. Ripped loose and set adrift in creation. The Gods had tired of mortals finding their way to the beginning, a place we were never meant to be, *shouldn't* be. Amkhira was already becoming confused when we spoke, losing coherence, forgetting who and what exactly they were. I knew that, if I had any chance at all, *any* chance, of escaping that place, the road had to be restored. I created the pink dolphin with a thought, gave it to Amkhira, told them to find you, and ...."

"Then you forgot."

He scrubbed the back of his hand over his eyes, wiping away the tears that had begun to form again. "I had to. Kept my sanity intact by imagining myself home, safe and sound." Father looked around. "And I know I'm not trapped there anymore. I know I'm free. My head is whirling right now, but nothing ... nothing's changed." He kissed my forehead. "Thank you for finding me."

"Don't thank me." I shook my head. "This is all Herbert's fault." Then I groaned. "We should probably make a stop before we head home. I have a delivery, and it needs to be made clear to certain parties that my pass into Zerzurrah is no longer valid."

Father frowned. "Why did you have to go to Zerzurrah?"

"Because that's —"

The road lifted in front of us, a ripple like an earthquake. The ripple curved into a half-circle, curling around us. We side-stepped quickly, moving to the right. The semicircle tightened, corralling us towards a narrow path that branched off Amkhira Street, stretching out into the darkness.

The ripple rose higher, the strange swirling golden-red circles and words stretching and undulating. Something glimmered, tumbled through the air, and plinked to the asphalt.

Father bent to pick it up.

The pink dolphin, the tiny cetacean Father had created from raw potential with just his mind and will, and which Amkhira had used to entice me into helping them.

Father shook his head, his smile almost wistful. "I wonder if this is a thank you or a you're welcome?"

"Probably neither. Amkhira is an inhuman entity as old as creation. I don't think they understand or have use for human manners." I turned towards the road that stretched off to our right. "I guess we go this way."

Father slipped the carving into his pocket. We stepped off Amkhira Street, and kept walking.

***

The reddish embers quickly disappeared behind us. They seemed to hover only around Amkhira. Everywhere else was darkness, and dark roads.

Eventually we came to another intersection. My hunch that these were crossroads seemed correct. I counted nineteen intersecting pathways, and the area felt … familiar. I could almost hear the echo of drills and diggers, smell the engines and mine runoff.

Jerseea.

We just needed to get … down … up … get there. Somehow.

I tried to recall how it had felt when I had fallen into Amkhira, when they had flattened and merged with the matter/mass/energy of creation; how Amkhira's red and gold highlights had spun and whirled into spheres and then flattened into circles, the road stretching out into infinity.

I needed to … um … reverse that. Flat to not flat, circle to sphere, within to without, everywhere/infinity to somewhere/finite.

Right. I could do this. I had to do this.

Rolling my shoulders, I made sure that I had a good grip on Father. "Ready?"

"Absolutely."

I started to inhale, hesitated, then said to him, "If I miss, or we fall, or get separated, or … anything. Go to Jerseea. Go to Herbert at Myss Lyla's. Tell him everything. Tell him I spent my pass, and there's no reason for anyone to come after you or Mother or Grandmother. Okay?"

"You're not going to miss. We're not going to fall or get separated. We're going home, baby girl." He gave me a single firm nod. "We're going home."

I swallowed and nodded in return. I turned my attention back to the intersection — the crossroads — focusing my attention on the where and the when I wanted to be.

"*Jerseea.*"

It hurt. It was like intraworld traveling with Amkhira when they jumped from one point to another. This was every color I had ever seen and a thousand more that I couldn't name, let alone imagine. It was a silence so profound that I could hear my own cells dividing and my synapses firing sparks of electricity. It was moving in every direction simultaneously without moving.

We stopped.

I was on my knees, screaming. My lungs wouldn't work right. I was screaming, but I couldn't get any air. Father was hunched over beside me, spitting up blood. His whole body was twitching.

"Fair welcome, one who is Walker Brown. One is grateful that you are not deceased, and that we may continue to engage in stimulating conversations."

I sucked oxygen, blinking rapidly to clear the spots from my vision.

Craning my head, I looked up to find Peterrmenn looming over us. His expression was solemn, his broad shoulders blocking out many of the street lights that encircled the Jerseea Crossroads.

"And a fair welcome to you, unknown traveler. Walker Brown, the Herbert has instructed this one to escort you to his establishment immediately upon your arrival."

I held up a hand, still trying to get enough air. My heart was thundering. I turned to Father just as he spat another wad of blood. He wasn't twitching quite so badly anymore.

He wiped the back of his hand over his mouth. "That was … not an experience I want to repeat."

I could only grunt in agreement.

Which is when I realized that it was *quiet*.

It was quiet. In Jerseea.

I looked around. The Crossroads were nearly deserted. There were a few Walkers, most sitting or kneeling, a few flat on their backs and sound asleep. Some glared at me, while others looked on in curiosity. Beyond the Crossroads, the drills and diggers and engines and hammers had fallen silent. I could hear the lights humming. The brothels, restaurants, courier stations, grocery stores, bars, temples — all shuttered, their windows dark, their doors closed.

"Shall this one carry you, Walker Brown and unknown traveler?"

I shook my head and pushed myself to my feet, my knees weak. "No, Peterrmenn, thank you. I can walk. May take a while, but I'll make it."

The Hemkirish nodded gravely, backing away a few steps.

"What happened?" I waved a hand at the silent city. "Why … this?"

Peterrmenn blinked slowly. "The Families await you."

Oh. That … oh.

"Father? Maybe you should wait here. Or, if you can't Walk, get a ride back to Detroit with another Walker."

"I'm good. Okay." He pressed his hands to the ground, grimacing, and pushed himself painfully upright. "And, as I said, *we* are going home."

I smiled and he grinned in return.

"In that case: Peterrmenn, lead the way."

***

The entire city had been shut down; or, at least what I could see and hear of it. Nothing moved. No transports or railcars. No music played. There were no shouts or laughter. There was no one. Just the three of us, moving through the quiet streets.

We passed a dark Sleipnir Delivery Services. There was no sign of Chinnis, not so much as a single eyestalk.

On a normal day, it took me nearly an hour's walk to reach Myss Lyla's. This trip was less than fifteen minutes, and the logo was visible from blocks away.

The buxom, four-armed blonde smiled down at us from above the front door. We crossed the threshold, leaving the smooth rock of the streets for the thick white, gold, and black carpet. I could hear soft music from the dining area, and the faint clinking of glasses and utensils; but no conversation, no laughter, no feet whirling across the dance floor.

The music skittered to a stop as soon as we entered the dining hall. The musicians on the stage gaped at us in surprise. The people seated at the tables all turned and stared.

I had never met any member of the Seven Families (Hemkirish, Human, Neanderthal, Felinian or Foxin), but there was no mistaking them. Exquisite clothing, exquisite jewelry, and that certain gleam of the eye and tilt of the nose that spoke of deep-seated arrogance and power.

No, I had never met any of the Seven Families, but I had met one of their representatives.

Baldy glared at me over the shoulder of a beautiful

Felinian female, a clove cigarette dangling between her bejeweled claws. The Mousekinth bite marks that covered his face were still red and raw, but a bandage now covered his torn ear and his suit had been replaced.

I stopped a few paces from the elegant, cloth-covered tables and looked straight at him.

"Ouch," I said.

His jaw twitched and he took a step towards me.

Father moved between us. "Hello, again," he said softly. "You owe me twenty years."

Baldy stopped.

No one moved.

"Well, as I live and breathe," a voice full of forced surprise and friendliness echoed across the room.

I dragged my attention away from Baldy and the Seven Families to find Herbert on the far side of the bar along the left wall. He had both hands braced against the sleek surface, the portrait of Myss Lyla peering down from the wall above him. He was smiling, but I could see the wariness in his eyes and the beads of sweat on his forehead.

"Jeremiah Brown. Welcome back," he continued.

Father turned slowly, his attention moving from Baldy to Herbert. He led me towards the bar, his steps slow and deliberate. He held out a hand and they shook. "Herbert."

"Good to see you again, Jeremiah." Herbert tilted his head in my direction. "I trust you were successful."

There was a fraction of a question mark hanging on that end of that statement, and everyone heard it.

Silence. No one seems to even breathe.

"I was," I answer, and pull off my backpack. I set it carefully on the floor, lifted the flap, and pulled out the ceramic cage containing the three hollow eggshells. I placed it on the bar top in full view of the gathered Families.

There was a collective inhalation. Excerpt Herbert, who breathed a sigh of relief. Some of the wariness left his eyes, and his smile this time was more sincere.

"Thank you."

I felt a corner of my mouth twist up into a grin. I leaned towards him, voice low. "So, what's the plan? Keep one for yourself and auction the other two?"

Herbert snorted, momentarily looking away to motion the band off the stage. "That a joke? They'd never let me out of here alive. No, we're all going to be very civilized about this."

He gingerly pressed one hand down on the top of the ceramic cage to hold it in place, wrapped his other hand around it, and twisted sharply. There was a snap, the ceramic splitting neatly in half. A server appeared with three cloth-lined gold and porcelain bowls and Herbert lowered one shell into each.

"They will spend their fortunes to make yet greater fortunes and shame their fellows, and I will happily walk away with their money."

This time, it was Father's turn to snort.

With a jaunty half-salute, Herbert walked to the end of the bar, following the server onto the stage. Every eye followed him. I had fulfilled my purpose, and was no longer of any interest. Only Baldy seemed to be paying me any attention; or maybe he was glaring at Father.

"Sirs and Siresses and Beings All, welcome," Herbert called out, and bowed. "An extraordinary opportunity now presents itself to you: the chance to own and drink from a whole Zerzurrahn eggshell, thus ensuring the continued health, prosperity, and luck of not only yourself, but also of your direct descendants down to the fifth generation."

I picked up my backpack as Father moved into my line

of sight, once again placing himself between me and Baldy. He led me towards the entrance.

"Shall we open bidding on the first shell at, say, ten million?"

Peterrmenn held the door open for us, tipping his hat.

"Come on, baby girl." Father wrapped an arm over my shoulder. "Let's go home."

"THIS IS UNNATURAL. UNHOLY, EVEN. QUIET IS NOT NORMAL."

I ignored Herbert. I had forgotten how warm and soft the sands of Millicent Island were, and I was stretched out on the beach now, my face to the sun and the sky. I was happy. Herbert was unhappy, therefore Herbert would be ignored.

"Are you listening to me?"

"No," I answered.

"Too bad."

I felt the thud as he dropped down to sit next to me.

"As I said, not normal. I need noise and movement and excitement, not *this*."

I cracked an eye open and say him gesture towards the still sea and the wide, cloudless sky.

"You could leave," I pointed out, and reluctantly sat upright. "Londinium, maybe. Or Fiorenzia. Pohjola?"

I crossed my arms over my knees, my gaze drifting across the beach. Mother and Father were walking along the edge of the water, holding hands, talking softly. Mother was crying again. Father shook his head, looking grim, and wrapped his arms around her. They hugged one another for a long moment, and then continued along the beach, still holding hands.

Branson had been the first to welcome him home. He had tipped his hat to Father, his face still cut and swollen, and held the door open.

"Glad to have you back with us, Mr. Brown," was all he said.

Word spread quickly. Within the hour, old friends and curious neighbors alike had stormed our trashed apartment: Aselolla, Judith and Judy, Shiranthz, Mr. Hogarth and all of his puppies. It had been overwhelming, and loud, and crowded, people stepping around the mess left by Baldy and his friends. Father and Mother finally retreated to her — their — bedroom, while Grandmother and I dealt with the crowd.

It had taken hours to get rid of them.

A vacation to figure things out had seemed in order. A long vacation.

And then a few days ago, Herbert had popped into the Millicent Island Crossroads, the portrait of Myss Lyla balanced on his head, and a massive bag of coins, credits, and gems slung over his shoulder. The Foxin Walker who had escorted him gave the giant painting one last dirty look and then disappeared back through the crossroads.

Nearby, Grandmother was building a castle. The sand here wasn't good for that. Sleeping, yes. Building, no. The walls would hold, but the towers kept tumbling down. Not that she was paying much attention to her construction work. Her gaze kept drifting over to Mother and Father, too.

"Pohjola?" Herbert huffed. "I think I would like wild forests filled with firefoxes and piru even less than I like *this*. Londinium has possibilities. Or maybe Kitezh. Buy myself a nice house with all that money. Start a business. Information broker, maybe? Not all that different from running a bar." He squinted at me. "What about you? Know any good secrets?"

I rolled my eyes and tilted my face up towards the sky again.

For a moment, it wasn't blue. It was infinite dark criss-crossed by dark roads. One road stretched on forever, covered in swirling red and gold circles and script. A tortoise walked that road, head and shell covered in circles. There was a great eight-armed elephant, too, a lotus painted on his belly, and an owl with a bronze helmet, and a rainbow-hued being like a praying mantis, but massive. A silver serpent longer than the sky whirled and danced, laughing.

"Bertha?"

"Hmm?" I blinked, and there was blue sky again.

The God, whichever God he had been, had been right. No mortal who gained a clearer vision of reality was ever the same again.

I wondered how much I had changed. How much I would continue to change.

"Career options," Herbert carefully enunciated.

"Later," I said. *Yes, later. Father, Mother, yourself. Worry later.* "For now, I want you to try something else. It's called relaxation."

His nose wrinkled.

I laid back on the sand, tugging him down after me. He fell back reluctantly. He squirmed in the sand, still frown-ing; crossed and uncrossed his hands over his belly.

"What do I do?"

I smiled and sighed. "Absolutely nothing."

About the Author

Rebecca Buchanan is the editor of the Pagan literary ezine *Eternal Haunted Summer*. She has published multiple short stories, novelettes, and novellas, which she is in the process of collecting, as well as two poetry collections, with more on the way.

A complete list of her publications may be found on *Eternal Haunted Summer*.

Novellas and Novelettes
The Adventure of the Faerie Coffin:
Being the First Morstan and Holmes Occult Detection
Asphalt Gods:
A Walking the World Adventure
Geek Witch and the Treacherous Tome of Deadly Danger:
A Tale of Magical Dice, Cursed Books, and Blackberry Jam
The Maiden and the Marrow Witch:
A Tale of Magic and Murder
The Secret of the Sunken Temple

Poetry
Dame Evergreen, and Other Poems of Myth, Magic, and Madness
Not a Princess, But (Yes) There Was a Pea, And Other Fairy Tales to Foment Revolution (Jackanapes Press)

Forthcoming
The Ballad of the Chalice and the Charm: A Tale of Friederich the Bard
Blood, Honey, Snow: A Tale of Murder at the Edge of the World
The Bones Are Walking, And Other Pagan Urban Fantasy Tales
Eleanor Tilney and the Black Dog of Beechen Cliff: A Hidden Regency Adventure
Grandmother Granddaughter Wolf, and Other Poems Fae, Fearful, and Fantastic
Jane Fairfax and the Siren of Weymouth: A Hidden Regency Adventure
Malkin: A Tale of Magic, Espionage, and Too-Curious Cats
Rueppelli and Yerik in the Great Bazaar of Repet-Yark: A Walking the Worlds Adventure
Vesta's Fire: A Tale of Roma Aeterna

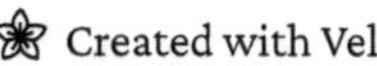 Created with Vellum